"THE HELLMOUTH," XANDER SAID WITH A GRIM SORT OF PRIDE. "KIND OF LIKE THE WHEEL OF FORTUNE OF EVIL CREATURES. YOU NEVER KNOW WHAT YOU'RE GOING TO WIN."

"I would not call it evil, exactly," Giles corrected. "Merely, well, malicious." He stood behind Willow, thumbing through his book slowly and comparing his source to hers.

Buffy shook her head. "Slight change of definitions, Giles. If it goes after humans, it's evil. End of story. And besides, it's giving me the creeps."

"Okay, so now we know what it is," Cordelia said so suddenly that everyone else started. Putting down her book, she glanced expectantly about at the others. "How do we make it go away? Because, you know, if it keeps hanging around, it's going to start killing people. They always do."

Buffy the Vampire Slayer™

Buffy the Vampire Slayer (movie tie-in)
The Harvest
Halloween Rain
Coyote Moon
Night of the Living Rerun
The Angel Chronicles, Vol. 1
Blooded
The Angel Chronicles, Vol. 2
The Xander Years, Vol. 1
Visitors

- Available from ARCHWAY Paperbacks

Buffy the Vampire Slayer adult books

Child of the Hunt
Return to Chaos
The Gatekeeper Trilogy
    Book 1: Out of the Madhouse
    Book 2: Ghost Roads

The Watcher's Guide: The Official Companion to the Hit Show
The Postcards
The Essential Angel

Available from POCKET BOOKS

BUFFY
THE VAMPIRE
SLAYER™

VISITORS

Laura Anne Gilman and Josepha Sherman
An original novel based on the hit TV series
created by Joss Whedon

AN ARCHWAY PAPERBACK
Published by POCKET BOOKS
New York London Toronto Sydney Tokyo Singapore

This book is a work of fiction. Names, characters, places and incidents are products of the author's imagination or are used fictitiously. Any resemblance to actual events or locales or persons, living or dead, is entirely coincidental.

AN ARCHWAY PAPERBACK *Original*

 An Archway Paperback published by
POCKET BOOKS, a division of Simon & Schuster Inc.
1230 Avenue of the Americas, New York, NY 10020

™ and copyright © 1999 by Twentieth Century Fox Film Corporation. All rights reserved.

ISBN: 0-671-02628-3

First Archway Paperback printing April 1999

10 9 8 7 6 5 4 3 2 1

AN ARCHWAY PAPERBACK and colophon are registered trademarks of Simon & Schuster Inc.

Printed in the U.S.A.

IL 9+

To Joss Whedon, and the cast and crew of *Buffy the Vampire Slayer*. Thanks for inviting us to Sunnydale. Only you could have gotten us to go back to high school—and enjoy it!

Thanks are due, and gratefully given, to:

Jennifer Heddle, for never even *threatening* to quit, Lucienne Diver (psst: tweed!), Peter R. Liverakos, the regulars at Malibu, the folk of JYGML, and everyone on #gasp, for being there when one or the other of us was losing it. And of course, our editor Lisa Clancy, and her assistant Elizabeth Shiflett. You guys epitomize calm under pressure. You scare us.

PROLOGUE

Buffy Summers took a deep breath of the night air and exhaled happily. Spring in Sunnydale. The air was fresh, the grass was growing—and the vampires were hunting.

Then again, the vamps never really do stop hunting, do they? It's not like they have game wardens or anything. . . .

"Now there's a job I'd like to see," she muttered, turning the corner and walking down a side street. "I'm sorry, Fangface, but your permit's expired. Oh yeah. Gotta remember that line."

The light from the streetlamps overhead was barely enough to cut the shadows, but she moved with perfect confidence. Muggers were not high up on Buffy Summers's list of Things to Worry About. There were worse things out at night in the town once known as Boca del Infierno, the Hellmouth.

1

On that thought, Buffy Summers turned around and confirmed that there were indeed two undead creatures of the night stalking her.

Or trying to, anyway. One of the few good things about being the Slayer, the one girl in all the world with the strength and skills, yada yada yada, was that it made it a major chore for anyone to creep up on her.

And she did mean creep.

"So, you boys going to dance, or are we going to stand here in one of those awkward who-asks-who-out moments?"

The vamp on her left hand moved forward at that, his snarl showing fangs that hadn't seen a dentist since, well, never. A round kick to the chest sent him staggering back a pace, giving Buffy enough time to pull a stake out and lunge forward to bury it through his heart.

"Tag, you're it!" she sang out, turning to deal with the second vamp. He came at her a little more warily, circling, trying to see if there was a weak spot in her moves.

But there wasn't.

As the second vamp burst into dust, Buffy froze. The slightest shiver ran across the back of her neck, where the strands which had escaped from her ponytail lay damp against the skin. It might have just been the wind—or it could have been her spider sense kicking in again, warning her of bloodsucking reinforcement on the way.

"Whatever," she muttered. "Come on, grave meat. I've got a history test tomorrow I might actually pass, if I get some study time in. So let's make this quick, okay?"

A heartbeat. Another . . .

Buffy let out her breath in the softest of sighs. "No? All right, then, guess not."

Tucking the stake away and wiping the last of the cold dust off her hands, she shook her head in disgust.

"One of these days they're going to figure out coming at me one at a time's a good way to make like a shish kebab. Remind me *not* to put that in the vamp training manual."

She looked at her watch, then considered the now quiet residential street. Enough world-saveage for one night. Time to go home and turn into Study Girl. As for that moment of weirdness after she'd staked the second vamp . . . Buffy shrugged it off. If there had been more vamps on the way, they had obviously gotten severe second thoughts.

Hidden in shadow, the creature grinned, a quick flash of jagged teeth, then slid silently away. The young female had an aura like none other, more hunter than prey—hunter, like itself, yes, but still human. *What human, what kind? Hunting down those drinkers of common blood, and without fear— so much power, so strong within her.*

But not so strong as to be invincible, never that! The creature shook itself in delight with a shimmering of shadowy fur. Drinking down that power, draining that strong life force . . . what a delicious thought!

Not yet, though. No. Not till it was certain of the bounds and limits of her strength.

No need for haste. There were so many other lives awaiting it in this new place. Life forces that would have no resistance to it, life forces to be taken so easily and amusingly.

And as for that one human, the hunter who would be one night the hunted . . . ah, yes! Even if the young female had taken the time to hunt a little more, she wouldn't have found anything. Because what had triggered her alarm had indeed moved on.

But it wasn't a vampire.

And it wasn't afraid of her.

Quite the opposite, in fact . . .

CHAPTER 1

"**G**ood heavens." Rupert Giles, a folded airmail letter still clutched in one hand, stopped short in the doorway of his sanctuary—Sunnydale High School's library—so suddenly that Buffy nearly crashed into him.

"Giles—"

He was looking about him in dismay. "The library is full of people."

"It *is* a library," Buffy pointed out. "People are allowed in here. If they want."

"Well, yes, of course. But normally, it is, uh, strikingly empty."

Which, Buffy suspected, was how Giles liked it. Empty meant that he didn't have to go through the motions of being a high school librarian and could instead focus on his true reason for being in Sunnydale. That reason, of course, was to be the Watcher to the current Slayer of vampires, and to keep an eye on anything else that happened to come visiting the Hellmouth.

Said Slayer being, duh, herself.

But today, the long low table at which the Slayer and her Slayerettes—Will, Xander, and Cordelia— usually sat, was filled with strangers: five chattering, gesturing fems and one guy, all a little on the old side to be your typical Sunnydale students.

Then again, Buffy thought, *what's typical around here? Werewolves, witches, invisible girls, Cordelia . . .*

The strangers' books and belongings were spread out across the table's polished surface as though they owned it. Not exactly *full* of people, but she saw Giles's point. They had definitely made themselves at home. A sight which did not give her warm and fuzzy feelings. *Her* library. *Her* librarian.

"Ah, may I help you?" Giles asked them all, shoving the letter he was still clutching into his pocket and doing a pretty good impersonation of a stuffy British librarian.

He doesn't have to act real hard.

"No, we're cool."

The young woman who'd spoken was striking, Buffy admitted, if one liked the snooty sort. A brunette, with a real I-am-the-leader 'tude. But natural, like she was used to taking charge, and people were used to letting her do it.

"Student teachers," Giles said suddenly, oblivious to the fact that he was standing there in front of them. "Of course. Principal Snyder was muttering about them all last week."

Buffy remembered now. Some new program from the local community college. One of those "real-life experiences" her mom was always so hot on, that usually involved extra credit and weekends.

Great. Just what we all need, more teachers. At least the invasion would only be for a few weeks.

"Hey Giles, Buffy says—"

Willow Rosenberg burst through the library doors and skidded to a stop as she took in the sight of the other occupants. Her face raced through surprise, dismay, calculation, and then a pleasant blandness settled over it like a mask.

Buffy had to give her redheaded bud credit—Willow was really getting the hang of that expression. Much more, and she'd be recruited by the CIA, as well as one of those take-over-the-world software companies.

Making an obvious effort to ignore the strangers, Willow added in a quieter voice, "Buffy says—oh. Hi, Buffy. You're there. I mean, here. Okay. I guess you can tell him yourself."

"I told you I was going to stop by and see him before seventh. You just forgot. She," Buffy said to Giles, "is obsessed."

"I am not!"

"Are."

"Not! Maybe . . . a little."

"Could someone perhaps, ah, clue me in?" Giles asked.

"The Battle of the Bands, you know?" No, the man clearly didn't, so Buffy tried the brief version. "Oz's band is going to be in a contest—lots of bands from all over the area—and that's all she's thinking about."

"I am not!" Willow protested again, more feebly this time.

"Are too. Trust me on this, Will. Your brain has turned into happy gray mush. And what I was going to tell you," Buffy continued to Giles, "is that I won't be able to make it this afternoon. It's, you know, Quality Time with Mom Day."

Once Joyce Summers had gotten over the understandable shock of learning that her only daughter was destined to spend her nights chasing down demons and turning them into dust, she had, Buffy thought, managed to deal well enough. For a card-carrying member of the mom union, anyway. The whole idea of a curfew for Buffy had gone out the window, which was a Good Thing, but a sit-down dinner at least once a week, complete with actual conversation, had been put into place with an iron fist.

"I see," Giles said. He left the newcomers to their own devices with only a single, worried glance, as though he was afraid they were going to start playing catch with his precious books. "Quite understandable. Despite the knowledge that the more people who know of your, ah, other responsibilities, the more dangers arise, I can't help but think that this is a good thing. Contrary to everything I've been taught as a Watcher, of course, but nonetheless, a good thing. You, um, will be, that is, you do still plan to study this evening?"

"Study?" Willow looked downright puzzled.

"Told you all she can think about is Oz and his band," Buffy murmured.

Red-faced, Willow said, "Oh. Right. *Study.* Lots of studying. After dinner. With her mom." Trying to change the subject, she added, "So, any new books come in?"

"No. Willow, I've told you already, I am not going to let you read any of the . . ." Giles looked over his shoulder at the student teachers, who were apparently immersed in their own paperwork—"the older books in the collection."

"You don't trust me," Willow said sadly. "He doesn't trust me, Buffy."

"It is not a question of trust," Giles cut in. "Not exactly. Ah, could we perhaps finish this conversation another time? I have . . . paperwork that I need to complete before Principal Snyder comes looking for me."

"Snyder? Here?" Willow squeaked. "Oh. I have class. Or something. Soon. Gotta go."

"Me, too," Buffy added, and hurried after her friend, catching up with her at the doors.

A low snort from the table in the wake of the two girls' exit indicated that a) the student teachers had not been as oblivious as it had seemed, and that b) they already shared the prevailing opinion of the principal after only a few days' exposure to him.

Giving them a quick, wary smile, Giles turned and all but dove into his office, closing the door firmly behind him.

Once safely alone, the Watcher sank into his broken-down chair, looking once again at the letter he'd retrieved from his pocket. And once again, a pang of alarm shot through him.

A member of the Council was coming here.

"Why?" Giles muttered. "Haven't we proven ourselves already? Over and over again, in fact?"

He glanced at the time . . . good enough. He could call England, demanding an answer—

No. If the Council is testing us in some way, panicking like that would send the wrong message. Better to treat this visit as a normal occurrence. A routine annoyance. No need to worry Buffy about it, either. She has enough problems right now.

Such as that dinner with her mother.

Giles snorted. He wasn't sure who to feel more sympathy for: his Slayer, or her mother.

"Buffy, it's not as though I'm asking you to devote your entire life to helping me out. Just one evening."

Buffy pushed the food around on her plate a little, not wanting to look up at her mother's face. It had been a really nice dinner up until this point. Well, okay, it had only been ten minutes. But setting the table had been fun. They'd even been singing along to the radio together, the way they used to.

"Mom, it's not that I don't want to. I know how much this opening means to you—"

"How can you know that? Tell me, Buffy. How many opening nights of exhibits have you attended? No, scratch that. How many shows have you attended, period?"

Buffy looked up at that, indignant. "Three. There was the really cool fabric thing from Japan, the African masks exhibit, and the West Indian whatsis that had the really weird food. Xander thought he was going to need his stomach pumped."

She sat back, triumphant. But the triumph didn't last long.

"The first one you attended because Willow wanted to go, and the second one your art teacher strongly suggested you all attend, for extra credit you needed to keep from flunking. And you all thought that the West Indies exhibit would have something to do with sun and sand and tanned guys in tiny swimsuits."

Buffy shrugged, contemplating the bit of chicken on her fork. "We had hopes. Your ads were false advertising."

"Buffy, all I want is for you to give me one evening of your time. An evening, mind you, that I'm telling you about two weeks in advance. I don't think that's at all cruel and unusual of me."

"I know, I know." Buffy wanted to help her mom out. Just not like that. The thought of standing around for hours, handing out canapés and refilling the punch bowl and making polite chitchat to art critics and newspaper reporters and people like Cordelia's mom, who was always anywhere there was Important Art being discussed—plus a few cameramen to take her picture, natch—made school look appealing.

"It's just that we had made plans to go to the movies that night, all of us"—no need to tell her that it would be Oz's last night of freedom before he went into the doghouse—"and I was really looking forward to it."

The Little-Old-Overworked-and-Highly-Responsible-Me thing was always a good bet. Her mother looked like she was relenting, just a little, and Buffy moved in for the kill. "It's not like I'm slacking off, or anything. Really. It's just that I need this break. It's not like I don't hold down a full-time job already. One, I might add, with horrible hours, no health benefits whatsoever, and absolutely no pay."

She paused, sidetracked by that thought for a moment, then decided that now was definitely not a good time to bring up the question of an increase in her allowance. "This was supposed to be the one night I got to dump it all in someone else's lap for a couple of hours and just be a teenager. You know, complete and total lack of responsible behavior? Can't you hire someone to help out? There's got to be someone who's good with that kind of socializing lurking around, right?"

Joyce Summers tried to be patient. She tried to be understanding, even with the added burden of being the Slayer's mom. But she wasn't perfect. And so she fell back upon the age-old cry of parents everywhere, in every generation.

"Buffy, honey, I'm not made of money. I can't

afford to hire anyone to help me out. So I'm afraid that I'm going to have to insist."

"But Mom," Buffy began again, spearing a piece of salad with unnecessary vigor.

"No, Buffy. That's final." Joyce sighed, finishing off her own salad. "Honestly, you'd think I was asking you to chop off your own head or something. I'm not asking for an entire day out of your life— just an evening. A few hours. And you can even bring your homework with you, so after we get everything set up, you can get some studying done as well before the press arrives."

Ouch. Bringing the grades thing in is fighting dirty. Buffy took a deep breath, trying to calm herself. This was her mother. This wasn't an enemy. This wasn't a battle.

"Mom. I'm trying. I'm busting my butt, in fact. You know that. And my grades are going up, so can't we ease up on the twenty-four/seven study thing?"

"No." Joyce tried to smile. "Tell you what. How about a bribe? You come help me out this one time, and I won't say a word about your study habits all that weekend."

Buffy chewed a mouthful of chicken and considered the offer. She'd make her mom happy, suffer for an evening, miss a night out with the gang, yeah, but a weekend free of mom nag? "Make it an entire week, and you've got a deal."

"Don't bargain with me, young lady. I haggle with art dealers who're tougher than half a dozen vampires every single day."

Her mom was joking, but Buffy knew that tone of

voice. It meant she'd pushed her about as far as was safe. Another whine, and the bribe would probably go the way of five-and-a-quarter disks.

Some times, even the Slayer had to back off. A little.

The moon was a pale sliver low in the sky, clouds scudding across it lazily. Buffy strode through the cemetery, Mr. Pointy swinging in a loose grip by her side. In a weird way, using the stake Kendra had given her made her feel . . . tougher. A little more able to deal with the weight of being the Slayer.

"Okay, none of that feeling-sorry-for-your-self stuff," she warned. But it was an easy thing to fall into. Will had promised to patrol with her, so they could do the study-talk and walk, but her best bud had bailed on her to watch the Dingoes practice yet again: the Battle of the Bands, as Willow had reminded Buffy at least five times today, would take place at the Bronze at the end of next week.

Oh no, she's not obsessed, Buffy thought. *Not much.*

Not that Buffy blamed her. Much. Hanging with your sweetie, even if he was totally involved in his music, beat stomping through the dead zone any night.

They're just lucky the Battle's set for a non-full-moon night. Otherwise there'd be that whole Teen Wolf thing to worry about. Gee, that would make the band really stand out, wouldn't it? Except—

She froze in midthought. There it was again—that cold prickly thing along the back of her neck that had been tailing her the previous night. Not the feeling she got about vamps, but ooky nonetheless. Buffy waited a bit, and it faded slightly.

Great, now I'm hallucinating. "I'm sorry, Giles, couldn't stake a thing 'cause I was jumping at shadows." Not a good way to start the morning report, no.

Not that there was going to be much to say. So far, the night had been a total bust. Not a vamp in sight, not even stupid ones. Just that weird feeling of being watched. And even that got majorly old after a while.

Much more of this, and she was going to start getting not jumpy, but downright bored.

Not that this is something I would be unhappy about. Mom's right: Bored is good. In small doses.

As Buffy moved on, she had an image of her mother, waiting up like she was on a date or something. *If only!* The social life was definitely in dormant stage right now.

A crackle of sound off to the left made her freeze. Something *was* watching her! Jumping up on a low monument, Buffy scanned the surrounding tombscape. Nothing moved, not even a stray cat skulking through the underbrush.

Geez, where is everyone? The mall? Is there a sale on I didn't hear about?

Shopping reminded her of the normal, everyday world. And that made her think of her mother again. Dinner, while good in a food category, had been a major ordeal for both of them. After they'd settled the question of the opening, things had pretty much fallen apart on the conversation side. How much can you talk about before you get to the subjects marked Do Not Mention in big red letters? Those subjects being Slaying, Slaying, and the ever popular Slaying.

Finally, her mother had practically booted her out of the house to go on patrol.

Which is just too weird. I think I liked it better when she didn't know. Kinda—

Something rustled right behind her. Buffy swung around into a fighting crouch, stake raised and ready for business—

But there was nothing there.

"Man," a voice said, "you are getting seriously wiggy."

Buffy jumped with a yelp and almost staked Xander.

"Hey, hey, hey! Down with the big splinter, Buffster. It's just me."

"You almost were wearing this!"

"Yeah, well, sorry. But I figured Will had Oz-ed out on you, which meant that you would obviously need company. And here I am, keeping-company boy."

"Cordelia dumped you, huh?"

"Sale at Neiman Marcus. Safer to hunt vamps than be around her right now. Uh . . . speaking of which, how *is* the vamp-hunting business?"

"Nothing. Nada. Except . . ."

"Except?"

Buffy shook her head. "I don't know. Like you said, wiggy. But . . ."

"But?"

"But I just can't shake the feeling . . . what, I don't know . . ."

"Hey, Buff, take pity on me, okay? Will you please finish a sentence?"

Buffy ran a hand impatiently through her hair. "I would if I knew what I was talking about! Xander, all I can be sure of is this: Something *is* out there. But right now, I don't know who—or what—that something might be. And—"

They both froze, then whirled. Something was definitely there for a second, though they couldn't see it clearly in the darkness, something big and seriously unnerving. And then it . . . giggled. A high-pitched, definitely not friendly giggle.

"What . . . ," Xander got out.

"Don't know," Buffy said grimly, getting a firmer hold on her stake and moving forward to find out.

But it—whatever it was—was already gone.

CHAPTER 2

Willow glanced about her with a contented little sigh. *Silence on all sides. Cool.* She had always liked the school library in the morning. It was quiet, with nobody here to make her feel even more awkward than normal. There was that nice, friendly smell of undisturbed books.

Besides, ever since Giles had taken over, this particular corner of the school had started feeling more home than home.

She spent more time here than home, that was for sure. And Xander was right, they needed a fridge. For sodas. And stuff.

Xander. A weird little shiver raced through her just then, and Willow told herself sternly, "Stop that." She was past that. Over. "Oz is my boyfriend. He makes me happy. And Cordelia really cares about Xander. I think . . ."

No. Stop it. Be happy with Oz. Sweet, totally unflappable Oz.

Oz and his band. Seemed he spent more and more time with them . . .

"Battle of the Bands," she reminded herself. "Only that. You get him back afterward."

With that, Willow took a sip of the herbal tea Giles had started stocking for her. *Nice, but . . .* She sniffed longingly at the scent of the Earl Grey rising from his mug across the table. *What if . . . ?*

"No, Willow," Giles said, coming back just in time to reclaim his mug. "I would prefer not having to explain to Buffy why I allowed you to get your hands on caffeine."

He stopped, the cup halfway to his mouth, and did a slight double take. "What are you researching there, Willow?"

"Nothing."

Of course Giles wasn't going to fall for that. He'd been around them too long to be put off by an innocent voice. Even from her. The Englishman moved quickly around to look at the screen over Willow's shoulder. She hastily minimized the browser, but he had already seen enough.

"Willow, I thought that we had discussed this."

"You said you wouldn't loan me the books. You didn't say I couldn't do research on my own."

He gave a long-suffering sigh. "I do wish——"

But before the Watcher could go into one of his famed lectures, the doors swung open and Buffy Summers stalked in, followed closely by Xander and Cordelia.

"We got problems, Giles," Buffy began.

"Big problems," Xander agreed. He jumped up on the counter and perched there, legs swinging, while Cordelia sat at the table beside Willow. But Buffy couldn't settle, pacing restlessly.

"There was something in the cemetery last night," she told her Watcher. "I mean, something more than the usual. Something not of the undead family. A big, nasty something. I couldn't see it clearly, but it was doing the menacing thing behind me. Stalkerish. And it, well, it giggled."

"Hyena giggle," Xander added, then shut up when Buffy and Giles glared at him.

"Seriously wiggy giggle," Buffy continued with a shudder. "And it was giving off some really bad vibes. Hungry vibes."

"Interesting," Giles murmured. "Definitely not a vampire?"

Despite her agitation, Buffy almost smiled. Giles was on the trail. Nothing made him happier than having some new weirdness to look up. She made a bet with herself, not glancing at him, then looked up suddenly. Sure enough, one hand held his glasses while the other was stuffed into a pocket. *Classic Giles Think Mode.*

"Not," she said. "Emphatically not."

"Didn't you see *anything?*" Willow asked.

"Nothing more than a shadow. I mean, I felt it, more than anything else. I'd been feeling it all night. And a little last night, too. Like I said, it was stalking me. But keeping out of range: this thing was definitely playing hard to get."

"But it made no move against you?" Giles pressed. "No overtly hostile act?"

"I'd say stalking's a pretty hostile act."

"And giggling? Sounds just like a freshman," Cordelia said with a sniff.

"Do you mind?" Xander asked her. "We're trying to have a serious bad-guy discussion here."

"Much as I am loathe to admit it," Giles cut in, "I must agree with Cordelia."

"Really?" Cordelia perked up, then remembered this wasn't a Cool Thing and began examining her nails.

"Yes. Well. Buffy, while I trust your, ah, 'spidey sense,' as you call it, there is no indication that—"

"Giles. Humor me, okay?"

"Right." He was suddenly all business. "We shall assume that this newcomer is of supernatural origin, based on your reaction to it, Buffy, and work from there. What do we have?"

"Giggle," Xander offered.

"Stalking tendencies," Willow added, already typing in key words for the search engine to use.

Giles nodded. "And a predilection for nighttime hunting."

Xander blinked. "Predi-huh?"

"It likes the night," Willow translated.

Cordelia glanced up from her nails. "And that makes it different from the rest of Sunnydale how?"

There was a moment's silence. Then Giles said, "Well. I suggest that all of you go on to your classes. I will do some research on . . ."

He paused, and Buffy continued, "Things that go giggle in the night. Right."

The lunchroom was serving meatloaf again.

"The question, of course," Xander said, dubiously poking the . . . stuff on his plate with a spoon, "is, 'Meat of what?' And why did they make a loaf out of it?"

It was raining outside, a gray, dismal dripping, which sort of spoiled the joys of going off campus.

"This . . . this is enough to drive a guy out into a tornado, just so he could get a Micky Dee's."

"Eww." Cordelia sniffed. "Don't eat it. Don't even play with it. Why did you buy it, anyway?"

"Scientific curiosity?"

He offered her a spoonful, and she shrieked and jumped up, smacking him on the shoulder.

"Xander. Leave her alone," Buffy ordered, poking at her own meal. She paused. "Did I just say that?"

"Say what? Hey." Oz appeared out of the seventh period crowd of mostly seniors, leaned over Willow's shoulder, and nuzzled her neck affectionately.

"Hey!" She smiled happily up at him. "Didn't think you were going to show."

"Busy time. We're doing that practicing thing, all lunch and free."

"Is it helping?"

"So far . . . it's not hurting. Except, maybe, my hands." He gave a brief demonstration of air guitar, ending with a wild riff. "Taking a break, letting the fingers heal."

Cordelia slid back into her seat before Oz could

take it, giving Buffy the cover needed to reach across the table and steal one of Xander's fries. "Do you know there are musicians all over the place? At least," she added, "musician wannabes. I mean, did you see the bunch over in the corner?"

"Krazy Klowns," Oz supplied. "That's the band name," he added hastily before Xander could comment. "Hey, look, the Battle of the Bands is open to *any* high school bands in the county. Awards, you know? Might be media coverage. Local paper, anyhow. Maybe even . . ." Oz shrugged, a little too casually. "Well, it's just a rumor, but there might even be a few record execs around."

"That is so cool!" Willow exclaimed.

"Rumor, only. But hey, it all means, yeah, we've got some wannabes, some garage bands who shouldn't have left the garage. But we've also got some pretty tough competition. You know, like the White Star Express or the Wizard Cats? And just now, I had to practically push my way through Don't Quit Your Day Job." He shrugged again. "So it goes."

"You guys think you've got a chance?"

"Not a bad chance. Not a good chance. Chance."

"Good thing it's not on a full moon," Cordelia noted. "It's not, is it?" she added, looking at Willow.

"Nope. We checked that."

"Anyway," Oz said, "gotta go."

"Go? You just got!" the redhead protested.

"Sorry. Deven's already got a bug up his butt about me missing practice three nights a month. We've got to use every minute."

Frowning unhappily, Willow watched Oz weave his way back through the crowd.

"That's the bummer of having a boyfriend in a band, Will," Buffy commiserated.

"Yeah, well." But then Willow brightened. "It's not like we don't have stuff to keep us busy, too. Like this stalker thingy. That's busy-making."

"Ooo, lots of fun there, Will," Xander cut in, pulling his fries away from the Slayer's reach.

"She's right, though," Buffy said, making a face at him. "We need to deal with this. 'Cause I'm not going to spend my nights looking over my shoulder for some creepie when I'm supposed to be staking the ghoulies."

"Aren't ghouls, like, dead things that eat flesh? Not drink blood?"

Everyone stared at Cordelia, who got seriously defensive. "What? You were all doing the Research thing. I needed something to read." She paused. "And, you know, Giles has got some seriously gross books in there."

Willow pushed her tray away and leaned forward across the table. "Okay. If it's a night hunter, like Giles thinks, at least we've got, like, time to deal with it. Right?"

"Right," Xander agreed.

"Not necessarily," Cordelia cut in. "I mean, just because that's the only time Buffy's seen this thing, whatever it is, doesn't mean that's the only time it's out. Maybe it's after Buffy, so it's out when she is. The better to catch her."

"Thanks, Cordelia. That's an idea I could have lived without."

"Gee, defensive much? I mean, you go around killing things, why shouldn't things come around trying to kill you?"

"Cordelia!"

That came from Xander and Willow as one.

"Sorry," Cordelia said, not looking very. "But think about it—"

"Shh!" Willow hissed, as two of the student teachers—the tall, skinny girl and that one guy in their group, a moderate hottie if you overlooked the teacher-wannabe thing—brought their trays to the unoccupied space at the end of their table.

"Is this space taken?" the guy asked.

"Um, no." Willow shot a helpless glance at the others, as if to ask, Well, what was I supposed to say?

The student teachers, pointedly ignoring the "mere students," continued their conversation, which seemed to consist mostly of "So I said to him" and "I hear you" mixed in with "So, what do you think about the way he handled that calc test?"

"I think we should maybe continue this conversation in the bat cave," Buffy murmured, looking uneasily at the newcomers. They might not have been teachers yet, but they *wanted* to be teachers.

Next to that, a midnight stalker that giggled at midnight was almost normal.

Outside, the rain continued, deepening to a downpour that turned the daylight almost to night. Not that the creature cared. Its eyes, after countless centuries of living in caves, might prefer the darkness, but there was nothing to keep it from hunting in the daylight. Now it stood motionless for a moment outside the walls of the huge building, wet hair plastered down, sniffing the cool, dank air, glancing about in the dimness that was no barrier to its sight.

Ahh, yes! The rain was sweet and full of a hundred little chirps and rustles as small things settled more deeply into the bushes. The grass was cool beneath the goat-hoof feet, the mud soothing. The creature giggled once, quietly, pleased.

A good place, this town, yes. So full of lives, nice, rich human life forces just waiting to be drained . . .

No. Tempting though it was to begin the stalk and torment of the prey this very night, hungry though it was growing to claim the first victim, drain the first sweet life force—no. *Not yet.*

First, much more engrossing even than the hunt, there was that one human who must be studied . . . the girl who moved through the darkness with so bright a supernatural glitter and no fear at all.

Just as she was doing now, there inside that cave of metal and brick. *But she will not stay there forever. No, not forever . . .*

With the softest of giggles, the creature settled itself to wait.

To wait, it corrected, *and then later to hunt.* Everything was the hunting.

And, of course, the feeding.

CHAPTER 3

There was something deeply satisfying about being somewhere one wasn't supposed to be. Ethan Rayne could think of several places on the globe where he wasn't welcome, but none of them had quite the same appeal of this aesthetically unpleasing but supernaturally enticing town of Sunnydale.

He breathed in the cool, slightly damp morning air with pleasure, watching the sun make its ascent over the hills rimming the eastern horizon and drying up the remnants of yesterday's rain. Ethan wasn't fool enough to enter the vicinity of the high school. Vampires were bad enough, but he didn't want to encounter that wonderfully irritating little Slayer.

"At least," he said, smiling, "not yet."

Not until he had a better idea of how best to annoy the Slayer, and her stodgy Watcher.

Oh yes. It would be a pleasant way to fill a few days, before he had to be in Los Angeles for his meeting. Always a nice little hobby, finding new ways to pester his old chum Rupert.

Filled with that agreeable thought, Ethan stretched one last time, then turned to open the rental car's door. But as he did so, squinting into the increasing glare, something made him pause. Caught out of the corner of his eye, a movement along the roadside, in the shrubs there . . . Alone, it was nothing. But Ethan Rayne relied on more than merely his five senses for information. And his sixth sense was feeding him a wonderfully tasty sensation of malicious satisfaction. A satisfaction emanating from whatever had just moved.

"Well now," Ethan said to himself once he was certain that the Whatever had moved on. "This could be interesting . . ."

AP biology wasn't one of Willow Rosenberg's favorite classes. But it was interesting, sometimes, and since she'd been able to get out of dissecting the pig fetus by doing a computer simulation instead, she didn't really mind it. She didn't mind the teacher, either. He was maybe Giles's age, kind of chubby cute, and a pretty good teacher in a seen-it-all way.

But there was class, and then there was being a guinea pig.

Behind her, Willow heard one of the boys whisper, "Think if we all turned our chairs to the left and stared at the other wall, she'd write *that* down, too?"

The "she" referred to the student teacher, the "ST" as Xander called them, a dark-haired one . . . Sheila Something . . . who was sitting just to the left of Willow's desk, taking notes. To be fair, it wasn't like there was much else to do.

"All right, class, let's see who did their homework." The teacher flicked the remote of the slide projector, and a new picture flickered onto the wall screen. It was a round segment, kind of off-white, with faint lines circling around inside. Willow frowned. Something about that cross section looked familiar. *What is it . . . ?*

"Anyone? No one? Come on, people, use those brains for something other than counting the number of tiles in the ceiling."

Silence, broken by a new voice.

"A unicorn horn."

Everyone turned to stare at the speaker—Sheila. The student teacher reddened and stared down at the floor like she wished a giant hole would open up and swallow her. But the bio teacher actually looked amused.

"Close, but no cigar," he told her. "This is a segment of a narwhal horn, a long protuberance that grows from the head of a—you guessed it, a narwhal. But these perfectly natural horns used to be represented as unicorn horns, and superstitious people claimed that they had magical powers. Now, who can tell me why a whale would have a growth like this?"

Willow looked at the slide again, then at the ST,

who was still blushing. *I have seen that drawing before.* In one of Giles's books. It *was* a unicorn's horn, she'd bet her new laptop on it.

But how had Sheila known that? Amazed at herself, Willow asked softly, "Excuse me? The, uh, narwhal horn—?"

"Of course it's a narwhal horn! I'm not stupid!" Sheila blushed even more. "I just, well, I'd heard the story before, about what people used to believe. That's all."

Gathering up her notes in a neat little pile, she pointedly looked away, focusing on the teacher.

Math was bad enough, but on top of that Ms. Sanderson always looked at you the way she'd look at a particularly nasty bug.

Or maybe it hadn't been bad enough, Buffy thought, *because now I have C. B. breathing down my neck.* Helpful C. B. the student teacher, the guy who had been sitting near her for this whole class, and not because he found her fascinating in a boy-girl way. No, C. B.—and how had she ever thought he was cute?—was oh so willing to show off how well he knew math—and how well she didn't.

Ha, surprise, she did know this equation after all! Buffy glanced up, and C. B. gave her his patented let-me-help-you-stupid-little-girl smile. She returned it with her equally patented wish-I-had-a-stake smile. Bingo! He tensed, frowned, and turned his attention to another student.

Score one for the Slayer.

Score more than one, actually, because she knew the answer to the next question as well. Maybe she'd get through this lesson unharmed. And maybe C. B. would, too.

Just then, the bell sounded, announcing the end of class and the start of her lunch break. Buffy snatched up her stuff and was out the door, escaping Math for Morons before Ms. Sanderson—or C. B.—could say a word.

Lunchtime, she thought, *used to be filled with the actual eating of lunch. And gossip. And normalcy.* Not that she really remembered days like that anymore, but . . . *Oh well. Deal, move on.*

She felt Xander fall into place beside her before she actually saw him, and knew without looking that Willow had joined her on the other side. Just like old times.

"Ewww . . . I can't believe she actually wore that in public!"

Well, okay, except for Cordelia being permanently attached. Although she's been . . . mellowing lately. Now there's a thought more frightening than the Hellmouth.

"We librarying it for lunch?" Xander asked.

"Are we ever not?" she answered, suddenly feeling more at charity with the world than usual. Giles would be there, nose in a book, getting her the answers. They'd find out what was stalking her, teach it some manners, and she could get back to her usual routine of slay, slay, and time out to party. Life was good.

Or mostly good, she thought, seeing a now familiar shape walking into the library ahead of them. "What do they do, sprint? I mean, to always be in there before us?"

This Invasion of the Student Teachers was beginning to be a major pain. They were turning up *everywhere* on campus, which was bad enough. But they especially seemed to be showing up in the library.

Worst thing was, they were all so . . . well . . . *nice.* She knew some of their names by now: Rebecca, the one with the curves that made Xander blink, superior C. B., who as the one guy had Xander insanely jealous, and the leader of their pack, Elaine. And Miriam, of course. She of the big brown eyes, devilish grin, and severe flirting. Miriam was the alleged reason that the student teachers kept winding up here, since the library was the only place that someone in a wheelchair could move around comfortably. Other than the cafeteria. And *that* belonged to the fencing team in the morning, and the chess team after school.

Gee. You'd think this was a real school or something.

But "alleged reason," 'cause Buffy had her suspicions about the appeal the library had for some of these unwanted visitors . . .

Sure enough, as Buffy and friends entered the library—ta-da, there they were again, four of the six. Student Teachers on Parade.

Willow sighed. "I used to wonder what it would be like to have a library that people used. 'Cause, the books and all."

"I don't think that some of them are all that interested in the books, Will," Buffy said dryly. "Just the book guy."

There at the main table, Giles had been roped into answering yet another question from one of the four STs who had set up camp there.

"Okay, gang. Time to head for Temporary Slayerette Headquarters."

The four teens changed course as a group, heading for the one secure place they could talk about stuff Slayer-related—Giles's office. As they passed, Buffy craned her neck to see past Giles and snickered. Sure enough, Miriam was batting her big brown eyes. Giles, as usual, was defining the art of obliviousness.

"That is just so . . . ewww," Cordelia announced. "I mean about those girls and Giles." She sat down at Giles's desk and pretended not to read the leather-bound book open before her. "He is way too old, and has, like, the lamest car in existence. How much do librarians make, anyway?"

"Older men with cars and money are okay then?" Xander held up his hands to deflect three sets of glares. "Just trying to get the rules all set in my male pea brain, is all."

Cordelia snorted, turning a page and paying a little too much attention to it for someone claiming not to read that stuff. The others made themselves as comfortable as possible, among the odds and ends and books that Giles crammed his office with.

"Man, you'd think Giles would take some of this stuff home," Xander grumbled, trying to make himself comfortable without knocking anything over.

"I think he needs it all here. For, you know, research stuff," Willow replied, having much less trouble fitting her petite form inside the small office. Buffy, coming in last, had no choice but to take the corner floor seating. Sinking into a graceful cross-legged position, she leaned carefully back against the bookcase. Satisfied that nothing was going to fall on her head, she let herself slip into what Giles called her grounded mode. Aware of everything, but not really taking in anything specific. Way useful in really boring classes, it was the next best thing to a nap.

"Still. I don't see why—"

The usual banter between her buds faded into background noise, and Buffy let her muscles relax. It was safe here. She *could* relax . . .

The tiniest beep caught Buffy's attention and pulled her out of her trance: Willow's laptop had just finished its most recent search. A few keystrokes, and Willow was reading intently. Buffy leaned forward and tried to make sense of the web page, but it was filled with small type and large words, and Buffy gave up.

"They need to make a bigger screen for those things," she said to her friend. Leaning back, Buffy pulled a magazine out of her backpack and started flipping idly through it.

"Umhmmmm," Willow agreed, her brain obviously elsewhere.

"We've lost her again," Xander announced, and then silence fell for a few minutes, broken only by the clicks of the keyboard, and the sound of turning pages.

"They say Leonardo's put on weight," Buffy finally said to no one in particular, studying a photo, "but he still kind of looks okay to me."

"Okay," Willow echoed absently.

"In a kid sort of way."

"Mm-hm."

"Give it up, Buff. She's not hearing you. Single-track-mind girl, that's our Willow when she's on the trail of something big."

Giles had finally escaped the clutches of the last young woman at the table, the light-haired one who always mumbled her name so you could never quite catch it. Joining them in his office, he gave a pointed glare at Xander's feet resting on the furniture. Xander hastily swung his legs down off the table and sat upright.

"Thank you," Giles said, moving carefully to avoid stepping on Willow, who was seated cross-legged in the middle of the floor. Reaching his desk, he evicted Cordelia with a glance, and sat down, picking up a small red-bound book and holding it open to one spot with his fingers.

"I believe that I may have found—"

"Got it!" Willow announced, her fingers finally stilled over the keyboard. "Oh." She looked up. "Sorry, Giles. But what Buffy saw. It's called a korred. It's—"

"A rather nasty creature out of Cornish mythology, yes. Furred, with cloven hooves and red eyes."

Giles paused. "I can see where it could easily be unnerving."

He seemed almost gleeful at the thought. *Hurray for scholarship,* Buffy thought, less gleefully. It wasn't sounding like something that would go away with a swat on the rear with a rolled-up newspaper.

"They're rather, well, tenacious, I'm afraid."

Nothing was ever easy. Buffy's good mood started to do the slow fade into grumpiness.

Willow, not to be outdone in the research thing, read off her screen. "Combining a nasty disposition and an intense curiosity about humans, it is known for stalking its prey and then . . ."

"And then what?" Buffy prodded. "Will? Giles? C'mon guys. Suspense is very bad for me at this point."

"And forcing them to dance," Giles said reluctantly.

"Dance? That doesn't sound so threatening."

"To the death."

"Oh."

Cordelia opened her mouth to say something, and then shut it again with a snap as a polite cough sounded from the doorway. Giles whirled, nearly crashing right into Rebecca, who took a startled step backward. "I'm sorry," the student teacher said in a voice that was anything but, "I was just wondering if you had a copy of the *Principles of Mathematics* textbook they're using for sophomore class? Mine is a dud—it's got a chapter missing."

It took Giles a moment to get the mask of "proper librarian" firmly back in place. "Yes, of course. In the back room. Just a moment, if you please," he added to Buffy and the others. "Yes," he repeated to Rebecca. "If you'll come this way, I'll get the book down for you."

As Rebecca, smiling, followed Giles out of the office, Buffy announced to no one in particular, "I could get to hate them."

"Which reminds me," Willow said. "Something weird happened in class today, with one of the student teachers. The dark-haired one, not Elaine . . . Sheila Something? She knew the slide Mr. van Deusen was showing was a unicorn horn."

"Van Deusen had a unicorn horn?" Xander asked. "Man, I knew he didn't date much, but—"

"A picture of one. And he said it was a narwhal horn, but it wasn't. And she knew that."

"Willow, there's no such thing as a—" Cordelia realized what she was about to say and stopped herself. "Is there?"

"Haven't the foggiest," Buffy replied. "Not caring, either, unless it tries to make like a menace. Come on, Will, she was probably making a funny. Or showing off."

"Maybe." But the redhead clearly wasn't convinced.

"Where were we?" Giles asked, hurrying back into the office. "Ah yes, the korred's means of attack."

"Dancing you to death," Cordelia prodded helpfully.

"Indeed. I assure you, dying from exhaustion is not a pleasant way to go." Picking up his book, Giles resumed his lecture without hesitation. "Although it is quite likely that a heart attack is the more probable cause of death . . ."

"Okay, okay, I get it," Buffy said. "Don't wear dancing shoes."

"Yes. Quite. Um, however, according to this, the korred is only slightly larger than your average gnome. So I am at a loss to explain the sensation you had of something larger."

"Oh. Here. I know that," Willow cut in. "It says that a korred can do that thing where it shifts mass, like, you know, a puffer fish. 'Cause size is scarier. To its victims."

"Hellmouth," Xander said with a grim sort of pride. "Kind of like the Wheel of Fortune of evil creatures. You never know what you're going to win."

"I would not call it evil, exactly," Giles corrected. "Merely, well, malicious." He stood behind Willow, thumbing through his book slowly and comparing his source to hers.

Buffy shook her head. "Slight change of definitions, Giles. If it goes after humans, it's evil. End of story. And besides, it's giving me the creeps."

He glanced up at her from the book. "May I point out that 'the creeps' aren't always a dependable reference?"

"You may not. Whatever happened to 'listen to your instincts, Buffy'? Or the ever popular 'the Slayer should know when something supernatural is afoot'?"

"I have never in my life said 'afoot,'" Giles retorted.

"Okay, so now we know what it is," Cordelia said so suddenly that everyone else started. Putting down her book, she glanced expectantly about at the others. "How do we make it go away? Because, you know, if it keeps hanging around, it's going to start killing people. They always do."

CHAPTER 4

$\mathcal{B}$uffy woke slowly, hearing something screaming at
her . . . no, it wasn't a scream, just the stupid alarm
beeping away. She reached out blindly, fumbling,
missing, finally hitting home, to shut it off.

Morning already? Way not fair.

She had kept waking up every hour or so, sure
someone was giggling outside her window—but
there'd never been anyone there. And then, when
she'd finally gotten some real sleep, she'd dreamed
that some shadowy, faceless creature was chasing
her, cackling madly. And when it caught up with
her, it jumped on her back as she ran, then
morphed into Xander with a quill pen, the kind
with the long purple feather attached to it. And the
feather had tickled the soles of her feet, making her
twitch, and she'd started laughing so hard she
couldn't breathe.

That was seriously bizarre. But not prophetic—just pepperoni.

One of these days, she'd learn to take Pepto *before* they ordered from Genero's.

Getting out of bed, she stretched and groaned. What was today again? Friday, right. For some other girls, Friday might mean the end of the week, time to relax and get ready to party. For the Slayer, Fridays were kickboxing practice. Buffy shook her head at the thought. This time she would really try not to do any more damage to her Watcher than was absolutely necessary. If Giles landed in the emergency room with a concussion again this year, he was going to seriously lose his health insurance.

So. Shower. Brush teeth. Morning stuff. Buffy snagged her robe off the hook on the back of the door and was about to head for the bathroom when her gaze fell on the textbooks sitting, unopened, on her desk.

Friday.

Math test.

"Oh no!"

The telephone rang at an ungodly hour of . . . Giles stared blearily at the clock . . . seven A.M. Watchers, like their Slayers, tended to be night owls from necessity, so it was a very unhappy Rupert Giles who fumbled for the phone, barely managing to wake up by the time the receiver made it to his ear.

"Yes? Hello?"

"Good morning, Ripper. Hope I didn't wake you."

Suddenly, the phone joined the computer and the VCR on the list of evil inventions designed to make Rupert Giles's life miserable.

"What do you want, Ethan?"

"What, I can't just call and see how—"

The patently false hurt in his former friend's voice was more than Giles could take this early in the morning. He reined in his temper with an effort and closed his eyes, still holding onto the receiver. "No. You can't," he replied, biting off the words. "What do you want, Ethan?"

"Just wanted to let you know that I was going to be in town for a few days. See if we could get together, have a few drinks, maybe talk about the good old days . . ."

"When hell freezes over, Ethan." And with that, he dropped the receiver back into its cradle and fell back onto the bed.

If he could have put Ethan and the vampire Spike in a room together, locked the door, and then conveniently lost the key, at that moment he would have done it. Without remorse.

Groaning, Giles forced himself to sit up and push the covers away. *Ethan's merely trying to shake you up,* he tried to convince himself. *He wouldn't dare come back to Sunnydale. Not with Buffy still actively looking to . . . what had been her words? Oh yes, "kick him until he bleeds."*

The memory made him smile. While occasionally impetuous, and regrettably prone—as all Slayers were—to using violence before words, Buffy did have an instinctive grasp for what the Americans called "frontier justice." *Quite poetic, really . . .*

Just then, the alarm clock began to shrill. Giles reached across the bed and slammed it into silence. Time, like it or not, to once again become Sunnydale High School's one-and-only school librarian.

But, he thought to himself as he got out of bed, *just because Ethan has always been a coward, there was no reason not to take precautions.* Perhaps he would make a check of the local hotels and motels, just to make sure his old friend hadn't decided to take the risk . . .

Willow glanced sideways at her friend as they walked down the school hallways, sliding through the noisy crowd like seasoned veterans of the mass chaos called period change. "So, I shouldn't ask?"

"You shouldn't ask," Buffy agreed glumly.

Willow's face fell. "But, I gave you all the notes, and, and . . ."

"And I'm sure they were good notes."

"Buffy. You didn't study?"

Buffy winced. She could face blood-hungry vampires, but a disappointed Willow was cruel-and-unusual punishment. "I know, I know. And I was doing so well on this school thing, wasn't I? But I was busy. Slaying. Watching for lurking gigglers. Kind of filled up my night, you know?"

Willow nodded her understanding. "Did *it* show? The giggler?"

"Nope." Buffy brightened. "But I did get this

really weird chickenlike thing that was crossing the road—"

Willow looked at her friend. "A . . . chicken crossing the road?"

"Chicken*like* thing, Will. Two feet tall, and teeth that weren't going to be used on . . . whatever it is they feed chickens."

"Other dead chickens," Willow supplied with scientific interest. "Ground up."

Buffy stopped short. "Will? Don't share this stuff with me, okay?"

Willow was used to the others not sharing her admittedly off-kilter interests. "Okay. Oh, I gotta go. I promised Mrs. Lee I'd stop by and explain that new database they're making everyone use for grading." She gave Buffy a quick smile. "One thing Snyder's ever done that doesn't make *our* lives miserable—just the teachers. And I could make a fortune, freelancing. Nobody's got a clue how the system works, not even the guy who installed it."

"Now, Will. Those powers of yours should be used for good, not evil, remember? Um—how much money?"

But the redhead had already disappeared.

"Great. Back to hitting up Giles for loans, I guess. They've really got to reorganize, make the Slayer gig come with a paycheck."

Buffy breezed into the library, tossing her bag on the counter. "Hi, I'm home!"

Giles, up near the stacks, looked up from the pile

of books he was reshelving. "Oh. Hello, Buffy. I take it this is a, um, free period?"

"Uh-huh. And so of course I thought I'd come spend it with my favorite school librarian."

"I'm the *only* school librarian," he pointed out.

"Details, details." She waved it away airily, walking up the stairs to join him. "Don't stomp on me, Giles, I've had a bad morning already."

"Oh dear. The math test?"

"Uh-huh. Major no-go. Let's move on to other, cheerier topics, okay?"

"Indeed. How was the hunt last night?"

"It might scare some people, Giles, that Slaying is what we consider a cheerier topic. And slow, that's how it was. Oh, but I now know why the chicken crossed the road."

"Excuse me?"

"No, Giles, you're supposed to say, 'Why did the chicken cross the road?'"

"Why did the chicken cross the road?" he asked obediently.

"To take a bite out of the Slayer."

Giles just . . . looked at her, as though unsure if he was supposed to laugh or not.

"Not a joke. Big chicken thing, maybe two feet tall. Teeth, wings—the whole deal."

"Chicken don't have teeth," he began automatically, then froze. "Good heavens! That sounds very much like a basilisk!"

"I didn't stop to get its name, Giles."

"Yes, but Buffy, you didn't let it meet your gaze?

No, of course not; you wouldn't be here now if you had." Giles settled his glasses more firmly on his nose and went directly to the shelf in the back where he kept all his personal faves. A Top One Hundred of all one ever needed to know about things that went bump in the Hellmouth. His voice came back through the walls of books, raised so she could hear him clearly. "A true beak? And what did its feet look like?"

"Beak, check. I didn't stop to count its toes, Giles. The thing was trying to have me for dinner. And not in the romantic way, either."

Giles had found his book, and was hunting busily through its pages so quickly that the parchment rustled. "Aha, there. Did your, uh, chicken look anything like that?"

Buffy glanced at the blurry woodcut, then shrugged. "Kind of. Things were happening pretty fast."

"Still. I do wish that you would remember to write down the details of any new creatures you encounter. You never know when something is going to turn out to be quite important, and if—"

"Oh goody. Tiresome speech about duty and responsibility coming up?"

That stopped him. "Erm, yes. Tiresome speech about duty and responsibility."

"Right. I'll go get the popcorn."

"Very funny."

"I thought so. Hey, Giles, could you loan me a twenty?"

The Watcher sighed, removing his wallet and

handing it to her with the air of a man who has done this so many times before, he's not even going to bother protesting. But, being Giles, he just couldn't let the moment go without a comment. "I don't recall anything in my training that indicated it would be my duty to act as your banker, as well."

"Hey, if I could get a job that pays, I would. But you and my mom have this thing about me going to school and getting a couple of hours of sleep every day. That kind of cuts down on how many hours I can stand behind a cash register going, 'Price check, please.'"

"Yes, I know. It's a terrible thing, to be dependent on such a pitiful allowance as your mother gives you."

"Okay, sarcasm heard and noted," she said to his back as he went into his office to set down the book he had pulled aside. For further research, natch. By Monday, he'd know everything there was to know about two-foot-tall chickens, and if she was going to have to make soup out of it or not.

Sighing at the unfairness that piled everything on her just as the weekend hit, she pulled out a twenty, wrinkling her nose slightly at the redesigned bill that looked like Monopoly money, and then did a double take, looking into the wallet again.

"Giles? Why do you still have pound notes in here?"

His voice, coming from his office as he continued a scholarly hunt, was muffled. "What?"

"Never mind."

Placing the wallet on top of the book cart, Buffy

went back down the stairs to put her bag under the counter. Security taken care of, Buffy leaned against the counter, enjoying the relative peace and quiet. For once, the student teachers who had pretty much adopted the library weren't gathered in a bunch, giggling and whispering like . . . like a bunch of teenagers.

"Gee, wonder if they're actually, you know, teaching a class?"

But even as she thought that, the door swung open, bringing with it the usual chatter and clatter from the outside hallway. *Great, there goes her quiet time with Giles.* And so much for the great chicken roundup.

Braced for Invasion of the Student Teachers, Part Two, she turned to give them all a piece of her mind.

The newcomer wasn't a student teacher. It was a man, maybe a little older than Giles. Dark-skinned, silver-haired, wearing a nice suit—good quality, but not too expensive, her mind automatically categorized. He carried a silver-headed cane, which was currently tapping against the side of his leg, emphasizing the razor crease in his slacks.

"Can I help you?" Giles would have been proud of her; she was being polite. But something about this guy was setting off alarms.

Or maybe you're just flipping out on anything new? Xander's right, you are starting to lose it. Calm down and give the guy the benefit of the doubt.

"I am looking for Rupert Giles?" His voice rose at the end of the sentence, as though he was asking a question. And there was the faint hint of an accent that she couldn't place.

Okay. Friend? Or old problem showing up at a really bad time? Giles, we have got to get a list from you sometime—y'know, friends who are okay, friends who need our help, friends who are really evil psychopaths in disguise . . .

"He's in his office."

"Ah. And you would be Buffy, yes?"

Okay, so that answers that question . . . maybe.

"I'm Buffy, yeah. And you are?"

"Forgive me. My name is Gerald Panner."

"And you're, what, an old college bud of Giles?"

"College . . . ah. No. We have . . . worked together before. I am a researcher. And Rupert has been most helpful in the past. So, being in the area, I thought I would, as the saying goes, look him up."

"Panner."

They both turned to see Giles coming out of his office, a small, red-bound journal in hand. He didn't look happy to see the newcomer.

"You received my letter, yes? So I am not a total surprise?"

"I received the letter."

Buffy sensed Go-Away-Buffy vibes in the air. Strong ones. And Giles was always griping about her not working hard enough on her other senses.

"Okay. So, you guys have lots to catch up on, right? Old books to reminisce about, all that stuff. So I'll just go now . . ."

"Yes." Giles didn't even glance at her. "Why don't

you go home, Buffy? We will continue our discussion tomorrow."

"Tomorrow's Saturday, Giles. Weekend, remember? I'll call if anything comes up."

"Yes, fine. Until later, then."

"Right. Not wanted. Leaving."

But she was already talking to herself.

Giles busied himself for a while in his office, clearing papers from a chair so that Panner could sit down, piling books more neatly on the desk and floor. Stalling. Knowing he was stalling. But—

"Rupert."

"I'll be right with you. Just have to see that this doesn't—"

"Rupert, please."

That was enough to get Giles's attention. Rare for Panner to show any degree of humility.

The newcomer moved further into the library, still holding his cane still at his side. "I am asking you to—what is the phrase? Yes, cut me some slack. I'm not here to cause you any discomfort. I am merely here as a researcher. Taking notes, as they say, by which future generations may learn."

"Research is a wonderful thing," Giles retorted flatly. "Especially since it requires the impartial observer to do exactly that—just observe."

"Why, Rupert, what are you saying? I am not here as a threat, truly, nor as a disturbance. Not even as a warning." Panner actually looked hurt. Or perhaps offended.

"No. Of course not. An *observer*." Giles knew his

tone was harsh, but he couldn't help the sarcasm that crept into it. He looked the Council representative—*no, call it as you see it, the snitch*—full in the eye for the first time and saw the man draw back ever so slightly. "Stay out of my way, Panner. Stay out of everyone's way. I assure you, we will all be much happier if you do."

CHAPTER 5

"**B**attle of the Bands Fever!" screamed the sign over the Bronze's door. "Open mike rehearsals today! Saturday afternoon special! Come early, come late! Music's still gonna be great!"

"Even if the poetry stinks," Buffy said, leaning forward to read the list of bands scheduled. "Oz, you sure about this?"

"Yep. Can't tell the players without a scorecard."

"No, I mean, you guys had a rehearsal here last night. Do you really want to spend Saturday afternoon listening to—"

"I think of it as penance for some really bad playing in a previous life," he said, taking Willow by the arm and heading inside. With a glance at Xander, who shrugged, and Cordelia, who merely rolled her eyes as if to say, "musicians," Buffy followed.

Overkill or not, Saturday afternoon or not, the

rest of Dingoes Ate My Baby were already in there, along with who-knew-how-many other bands—almost all of them taking notes about the sound, or jeering at their competition.

"Battle of the Bands," Buffy said under her breath as they grabbed a table off to the side of the stage. "Why does that phrase suddenly give me a bad case of Uh-Oh?"

"Because we live on the Hellmouth?" Cordelia asked.

Sometimes, Cordy really just made too much sense.

Someone had finally managed to update the Bronze's sound equipment. Or maybe they'd just finally kicked the amps in the right spot. Buffy leaned forward, trying to ignore the crowd around her and listening as critically as she could to the band currently onstage.

They're good, she thought with some dismay. Really good. Good enough that the noise level in the Bronze had toned down to where you could almost hear yourself talk without yelling.

The lead singer, seriously cute, went for and actually hit a high note, then followed that triumph with a lightning-fast riff on his guitar. Buffy leaned back and sighed, and not because of the way his jeans fit. *Well, not totally.*

Really good band, all right.

And unfortunately, they weren't Dingoes Ate My Baby. The White Star Express, and they'd already had more gigs, more paying gigs, than Dingoes, too.

Beside her, Willow was looking more and more cheerful, in the desperate sort of way she had when things were going downhill. "You can play that riff better," she assured Oz.

He shrugged, classic Oz. "Guy's not bad. The whole band's not bad."

Xander snorted. "Yeah, but can you dance to it?"

Cordelia, ever tactful, turned to Oz. "Aren't you worried? I mean, they're obviously better than you."

"Oh, way to go, Cordy," Xander muttered under his breath, no longer wasting energy trying to clean up after Cordelia's artlessly rude comments.

But Oz just shrugged again. "Why? We lose, we win. Equal stuff either way."

"That's so mature of you," Willow said admiringly.

Yeah. Right. Mature. The rest of Dingoes, Buffy noticed, weren't managing the mature thing so well.

"Missed the chord," Devon muttered with malicious satisfaction.

"Yeah," another member snickered, "and drummer's not in sync; he's throwing them all off."

"It's your stupid voice that's throwing everyone off," a guy snarled at him, and Buffy turned.

This guy *had* to be a lead singer. Mr. Macho, all fake black leather and fake silver chains.

"Boys will be boys," Buffy said in Willow's ear, watching the posturing with the practiced eye of a trained fighter.

Sure enough, the Dingo he'd confronted took the bait, standing up and trying to loom over the other guy. "Maybe it's your lack of talent making all the noise."

Both guys were on their feet now, obviously looking for a chance to butt heads, and others were starting to get up as well.

"Eeeeep." That came from Willow, who was looking around, her big eyes even wider. "Fight. Bad thing."

"Whoa." Oz got casually to his feet, moving between the two guys. "Not worth it."

That got scowls from both sides. "Not worth what?" someone yelled.

Oz shrugged. "Giving the town council an excuse to shut this place down. They only need one."

Buffy hastily backed him up. "Snyder thinks the Bronze is a 'den of iniquity' anyhow. He thinks we're all plotting in here to ruin his perfect-attendance scheme."

That got a laugh from everyone who'd ever run into the principal. Willow gave Buffy a quick grin. "Sounded just like him."

"I know. Scary, isn't it?"

Oz was saying something to the rest of his band. With reluctant shrugs and glances over their shoulders, they moved off. And after a few seconds of muscle twitching, the other band members sat back down again, too.

Xander glanced at Buffy. "Battle of the Bands. You got that right."

Buffy sighed. As if she didn't have enough with the Midnight Giggler and a Slayer's nightly—and nonpaying—job, now she had to wonder if the one real teenage part of her life was going to get shut down for extreme violence and conduct unbecoming upper-middle-class children.

The first guy to start a fight in here, she decided, *is really, really going to be sorry.*

The small motel room had seen better decades. "Dingy" would have been a polite way of describing it: peeling yellowed paint, worn curtains pulled against one dirty window, a carpet of some nondescript color and material, and the smell of mildew hanging heavy in the air. But the front desk took cash and didn't even bother asking for names, which made it perfect for Ethan Rayne's purposes.

At the moment, he was seated on the narrow bed, having pulled the sheets off and tossed them into a corner. Legs crossed, he contemplated the several small piles of herbs on plastic sheets in front of him with calculating satisfaction. Herbal magics weren't his strong point, but needs must . . .

"Valarian, for calming," he said, "clover, for softening the will, and marjoram to entice. Maybe something for a good mood—no, best not. You never know what a good mood will do to creatures. Might make it hungry."

A few quick sightings had been enough to confirm his suspicion that his quarry, whatever it was, was lower on the magical food chain than he, himself. With the right ingredients, Ethan was sure he could create a spell to both lure the creature to him and, more important, make it docile to his commands. Or at least agreeable to them. With magical creatures, it was always best to try bribes before coercion. Less chance of irritating something with a long memory.

Of course, Ethan thought with a momentary chill, *I also run the risk of inviting in something I don't want.* A very real risk in this town, where assumptions could get one hurt.

Right. Once he had the details of the spell settled, he would need to find a perfect place. Neutral territory, where he could make a hasty retreat if needed. That was, after all, how he'd survived all these years. Planning for every possible outcome.

Ethan looked at his watch, then plucked a pinch from each pile and mixed it with a handful of dry brown dirt, then carefully placed the entire mess in a small square of unbleached muslin, wrapping it securely. Getting to his feet and reaching for his jacket, he deliberately misquoted, "If 'twere done at all, 'twere best done before midnight," and left.

The white van with the red cross painted on the side drove out of the darkness and pulled up to the emergency room door, caught in the glare of the overhead lights. Blood bank delivery night, right on schedule.

"You'd think they'd learn by now," Buffy muttered from where she stood, watching. "Try to vary the times a little. Maybe not broadcast when they're coming in? But no, they've gotta run like clockwork, no matter how many shipments they lose."

Although, she was pleased to note, they hadn't lost many since she came to town.

Not that the vamps didn't keep trying. And there they were, right on schedule, too.

The trick here was to stay in the shadows while staking the vamps before the vamps got the techs or before anyone who happened to be looking out a hospital window saw a blond teen stabbing a man—a man-shaped thing, anyhow—who promptly turned to dust.

No one ever said the job was going to be easy!

Buffy snuck up on a vamp, one who'd been a solid, almost-square-shaped woman when she'd been alive, and tapped her on the shoulder. The vamp turned around with a snarl.

"Candygram," Buffy said, and struck.

One down.

Another two were coming in behind her. She stood, weight on the balls of her feet, knees slightly bent, waiting for—*now*. Buffy whirled, lunged at one vamp with stake in outstretched hand, making him stagger back, then kicked the other hard enough to make *him* stagger back. She staked the first before he could recover his balance, sensed the other looming up behind her, ducked under his grasping arm, and stabbed back and up—

Two more down. Any more?

Nope. Light load tonight. That'd make Giles feel better—he was following up on some lead or another, but he really hated her doing this part of the job alone.

Although what he thought he could do, really . . .

Oh well. He wouldn't be Giles if he didn't fret. But that was done, and in record time, too. She'd be able to make it to the cemetery in time to see if—

Then Buffy felt that all too familiar prickling at the back of her neck and heard that all too familiar giggle. She dove into the shadows, stake clenched in her fist, trying to locate the source of the sound. And as she hunted, Buffy could swear it wasn't a true giggle anymore. It was just one short step from being a snarl. Almost as though the Midnight Giggler was finally growing tired of just watching.

"Yeah. I'm snarling, too. Let's have this out, stupid, okay? Just one little fight, winner takes all."

Nothing. Suddenly even the eerie prickling at the back of her neck was gone.

"Coward," Buffy muttered.

Yeah, but cowards usually went on to beat up on someone weaker than themselves. *Great. Just great.*

The korred stood in the deep shadows, shivering. It wasn't cold; it didn't mind a little damp edge to the air. Something was pulling at it, something prickling along its nerves, a pull, a call, a whisper, making it restless—

And hungry.

The korred shivered again, its hair moving with a life of its own, reddish brown in the uncertain light. Yes, it still was drawn to that one young human girl who glimmered with strength. But . . . it would not even try to snare her. Not yet. Not till it had enhanced its own strength. Not until it had fed.

It sniffed the air, then wrinkled its nose in disgust.

These humans insisted on covering the earth with hard surfaces and filling the air with harsh smells. Their houses stood each by each, with mere squares of green guarded by silly little fences. Trees were fenced in, too, each separate from the next, giving the korred little room in which to hide. Yet it needed little room; shadow was enough, and this neatly trimmed row of bushes . . .

There!

It crouched low to the ground, hidden behind the bushes, waiting with a predator's patience. A girl was approaching, arms full of packages and walking with the casual ease of prey that has not a hint it's being stalked. The korred had never seen this young human before, but that didn't matter. The glow in her was fresh and full of energy, and the korred drew back its hard-skinned lips in a pleased grimace. It followed her for a time, silent as the shadows, until at last they left the straight rows of houses—with their possible human observers—and came out onto a wider square of grass.

No witnesses here. Straightening soundlessly, still shrouded in shadow, the korred began the softest hint of melody. The girl stopped, frowning, listening to the music she could almost hear. She stirred, the faintest of dance steps. Another. It almost had her, almost—

"Hey! Karen, wait up!"

The korred started, melody faltering for an instant, too dazed by the sudden interruption to move. But then, with a silent snarl of fury, it sank back into hiding. It could have snared one or even two humans. But here came a herd of young humans, laughing and chattering—yes, and one of them was carrying a black box blaring its own music, which hurt the korred's sensitive ears.

As the raging korred watched, he saw the girl laughing with the others, all of them unaware of how close she'd come to her death.

The korred hissed, a low and angry sound. It had been foolish in coming this far into the town. True, there were fewer humans in the secluded places— but a wise hunter did not hunt the prey so close to the prey's own lair!

Foolish. But not defeated.

This time, the prey escaped.

Soon enough, another would not.

Chapter 6

Sunday, tranquil Sunday. *A little slice of tranquility is nice,* Buffy thought. Particularly when her sleep, when she'd finally gotten to sleep, had been full of dreams of giggling shadows—with sharp, glinting fangs. Once, she'd even gotten out of bed and prowled around outside, sure she'd felt the warning prickling of danger, but there'd been nothing menacing out there.

And the day so far had been actually normal.

As normal as Sunnydale got. Buffy glanced at the clock. Eight-thirty. Still plenty of time before she had to start her Sunday evening patrol. In the meantime . . .

In the meantime, we have a greater enemy to face. The weekly sorting of the laundry.

"Whites, there. Delicates, over here," and she threw a Lycra bodysuit on the bed, to join a small pile of hand-washables, "and hot water stuff over to you."

Her mother caught the pair of pants with one hand, dropping it into the pile growing by the door. "Nice to see you haven't lost all touch with your domestic side."

"Hah. Why can't we just pile all this into the car and drop it off at the dry cleaners? Xander says that's what his mom does. Of course, the way Xander dresses, maybe that's not such a good idea either. It might all be an evil plot on the part of the dry cleaners . . ."

Joyce Summers hesitated a moment. "That was a joke, wasn't it?"

Buffy sighed, looking up at her mother with affection. "Yes, Mom. Joke. As far as I know, dry cleaners are just part of the evil conspiracy to take our money, nothing else."

"Oh. I just wanted to make sure."

Coming farther into the room, carefully stepping over piles of dirty clothing, her mother sat on the edge of the bed and stitched a desperately cheerful smile onto her face.

Uh-oh, Buffy thought. That meant Slaying stuff. It was still new, this Knowing-About-Buffy thing, and neither of them had figured out how to start conversations about it without a lot of dancing around the subject.

"So, Buffy." Judging from her mom's equally cheerful voice, she was going to try to nonchalant it out. Well, points for trying something new. "How was, um, the slaying last night?"

Buffy glanced at her, not sure what was safest to say. "Quiet," she said at last. "Made sure the hospital got its deliveries. No trouble. Then, well, I spent most of the night going over math proofs again with Willow. She's just like this little logic machine."

"That's true. That's really true. Quite a bright young woman, Willow. I'm sure she'll be able to name her own price when she graduates from college."

"Yeah. I bet."

What Buffy wasn't about to tell her mother was that the tutoring session had gone on outside the morgue, while they waited for an out-of-town businessman to rise. That was one guy who wasn't going to have to file an expense report ever again.

After that, she had done one last swing through the graveyard, just to make sure nobody was partying without permission. But there hadn't been another vamp in sight. Saturday night vamp holiday.

A holiday. Sure. With someone getting his, her, or its fun out of watching her. Stalker's Delight: Slayer to go. At least there hadn't been any more of those stupid giggles since that giggle-snarl at the hospital. It must have figured that it was being way too obvious. The local radio station, with its news of sports and weather, hadn't slipped in any bits about any sudden deaths.

"Well, I'm glad to see that you're taking your homework so seriously," Joyce continued, "to study on a Saturday night. You do realize that you have a lot to catch up on."

Oh, rub it in a little, why don't you, Mom?

With that one last little prod, her mother stood, the conversation, thankfully, over. But then she stopped, thinking back over what Buffy had said.

"Ah, Buffy? 'Quiet,' you said. Is that . . . normal?"

"Mom." Buffy had to laugh. " 'Normal' and Sunnydale don't really go hand in hand, if you hadn't noticed." She hesitated, wanting to tell her mother about her stalker. But one look at Joyce's face, the dark shadows under her eyes that had never really gone away since the events of last summer, and Buffy couldn't do it. She and Giles had told her mom a lot—but there were some things it just wouldn't help any to share. And it probably would hurt. "I'm sorry, Mom. There just isn't anything else I can tell you."

Joyce didn't try to argue. She nodded, then her hand reached out to stroke the top of Buffy's head, and the Slayer leaned into that touch for just a second. A nice, normal, too-fast-for-a-Kodak-Moment instant between mother and daughter.

Then her mom was gone, leaving her with a pile of whites and colors and a sharp little inside-the-mind sort of pain.

The korred stalked lightly after its prey, the blades of grass barely bending under its goat feet, following the so-intriguing human, trying to ignore the prickling pulling at it, rousing its hunger anew. It could so easily lose itself in thoughts of silly, helpless humans who would writhe and twitch and dance dance dance . . .

Would it be able to snare this one human as well? Would it feed on her essence as it fled her body?

Not yet, not yet. It had still to puzzle out what was so different about her . . .

But then it stopped short, alert and tense, listening, sniffing the air . . . yes. There was someone else out here this night as well, not truly human, someone who might spoil all the fun.

With one last look, it faded into the darkness.

The night was cool and damp, so late that the moon had set a long time ago, and there was that almost gray on the horizon. Almost dawn, in fact. Buffy hesitated, wondering why she was still hunting when any self-respecting vamp would have long ago called it a night. All right, so she'd stopped by Will's for a while. But it hadn't been *that* long.

As for the Giggling Stranger . . . not a sign of him, her, or it, either, which might mean—she didn't know what it might mean. Hopefully, that the critter had gotten bored and gone away. Also hopefully, that the critter hadn't decided to go and catch itself some human prey . . .

"Nope. Not going there. Don't think about what you can't help. Think about the good parts.

"Right. The good parts. Like . . ."

Okay, so there was the advantage of weekend slayage, getting to do the sleep-in thing. *Always a plus. Any other pluses?*

Buffy thought for a moment. "Nope. That's about it."

And since it was currently Sunday night—well,

Monday morning—she didn't even have that to look forward to. Made one thankful for lazy Sunday-afternoon naps . . .

The scritch of shoe leather on pavement made her whirl around, but even as she was raising a stake, she recognized the figure in the shadows. And her heart gave a great leap.

Ohgodohgod . . .

"Angel." That came out normally. "Didn't expect to see you around here."

Good. Her voice was staying nicely cool. Not unfriendly, but not welcoming either. *You could frost glass with the cool.* But if he felt it, it was totally inside. Outside, he was Cryptic Guy again.

"There's something in town," he said without any sort of greeting. "Something new. Or rather, something very old. It doesn't belong here. Might be trouble."

"Late-breaking news; already known." Buffy lifted one shoulder in as casual a shrug as she could manage. "Don't worry, we're on it."

The cool was slipping. Trying to joke, Buffy added, "You know, the job description said 'vampire' slayer. Think I can sue for misrepresentation? But then, Giles would get bored without these fun little research parties. Him and Willow. And Cordelia. She's starting to scare me. Do you know, she actually knew what a ghoul was? Someone needs to tell her that knowing all that stuff's bad for the complexion, or something. And I'm babbling, so I'll stop now."

He fell into step beside her, matching her stride.

But a careful distance remained between them. They both noticed it. Neither one moved closer.

Neither one moved further away.

"We can handle this," she said, finally. "Me and the gang, that is. We've gotten pretty good at this. And it's not quite on the same level as saving the world. At least, Giles doesn't think so. Yet."

"I worry." It was barely more than a whisper. "I can't help it. I can't stop."

Ease up on the angst-o-meter, as Cordelia would say, Buffy thought. *This isn't easy for me, either, in case you missed that little fact.*

"Yeah," she said out loud. "But you stay away so it doesn't show so much, is that it?"

"What do you want me to do, Buffy?" His voice rose, his emotions cracking through the chill mask just the smallest bit. "Do you want me to stay? Do you want me to go away forever?"

"Yes," she said softly, not making it clear which option she meant—not so sure about it herself—and he sighed, defeated.

"Angel . . ."

"Be careful, Buffy. I knew creatures like this invader when I was . . . a long time ago. Don't belittle it. This thing is mean. Be careful."

"I always *plan* to be careful," she said—speaking now to the empty shadows.

"But," she added very softly, "sometimes I just don't get a choice."

CHAPTER 7

It is, Ethan Rayne thought, *much too early in the morning.* So early that dew still spangled the grass, etc, etc, and the sky was just starting to show color. So early, in fact, that he was seriously considering giving up this whole business and going back to bed.

In that disgusting excuse for a hotel?

On second thought, it was worth a little discomfort—the operative word being "little"—to both disconcert the Ripper *and* gain himself a potentially useful supernatural . . . pet. He had definitely contacted it on Saturday night, even though he couldn't hold the contact and was too tired to do anything about it on Sunday.

Now, though . . . Trying not to wince at the chill, Ethan settled himself on the bare rock he'd found. Granite, unusual in this land of limestone, and as magically neutral as he could find. Carefully unwrapping his chosen herbs, Ethan began his spell . . .

Willow frowned, looking about at the impatient group of students in the classroom around them. "You think someone maybe locked her in the bathroom, or something?"

Buffy shook her head, trying to stifle a yawn. "No way. The walls are so thin, you could hear her yelling." She suggested in turn, "A long-lost relative left her money and she quit?"

"Nobody here gets that lucky. Oh, no, I've got it! Snyder finally lost it, and started foaming at the mouth, and he bit her, so she's gone to the hospital."

"Ooo, I like that one," Buffy said approvingly. "You always get those details in."

Willow blushed and shrugged. They were playing the old school game of Where's the Teacher? So far, Ms. Ellis was ten minutes late for seventh period. Rules said you had to wait for twenty minutes before class was called on account of teacher no-show. Of course, they *could* have gone and told someone they were teacherless.

Yeah right, Buffy thought, watching two more students decide that they had better things to do and slip out the classroom door. *Like that's going to happen. Odds are, they'd stick us with one of the student teachers, and they'd be so maddened with power they'd actually try and give us homework, or something.*

Xander had suggested that they leave as well, about three seconds into the no-show. Buffy had been all for it, but Will hadn't been real big on that idea. Something about unexplained absences and a desire to see Buffy actually graduate. And, anyway, if they had shown up in the library when Giles knew for a fact they had class . . .

No, Willow was right. Better to hang here. No need to give her Watcher any new excuse to fuss.

And when did my idea of cutting class turn into hanging in the library? That's as pathetic as anything Cordelia ever gave abuse for.

But it wasn't easy to just sit here. Last night, after she had finally been able to go to bed, Buffy had heard that stupid giggling again. Surprise, surprise, when she'd dragged herself out of bed to hunt, she hadn't found anyone. And when she'd gotten back into bed again, it was to dream that she was trying to stake a shadow that kept whistling at her.

Not a good way to get some quality rest.

I have got to find that critter and kick the giggles out of it. Yeah, and instead of sitting here, we should be looking through the books and Will's computer files, make sure no one got the dancing blues last night while I was—

"Oh, hey, did I tell you?" Xander asked, leaning forward in his chair, and Buffy nearly drove an elbow into his ribs before she realized who it was. "Hey, jumpy, aren't we?"

"I just don't like loud noises in my ear, okay? Even when the sun's up and shining."

"Sure. Listen, I think I've got a line on a job. Money for Bronzin', here I come!"

"That's cool," Willow said admiringly. "Where?"

"And is that why you were saying those words over and over again to yourself?" Buffy asked. "Auditioning?"

Xander stared blankly at her. "What words?"

" 'You want fries with that?' "

Willow giggled, and Xander put on his hurt face. "You mock me."

"I see target, I take aim, I achieve scorage. It's a simple equation, but one that gives me a happy."

"Sure, mock all you want. But the job market is not a pretty sight around here. Even less when your sole marketable skills revolve around dead things."

"And obscure ways to kill people made of bugs," Willow added helpfully. "Don't forget that. 'Xander Harris, Exterminator. No night calls, please.' "

"Now there's a depressing thought," Buffy said. "Do you realize that I have absolutely no marketable skills? Except working out. And beating bad guys up. Hey. I could become a personal trainer."

Willow blinked at her. "You need to get, like, a dietician's license, or something, to do that, don't you?"

"Oh." Buffy sank back down into her seat, her enthusiasm notably muted. "More school. Great."

Just then, the door swung open, and Snyder walked in, followed by—

Buffy groaned. Yeah, one of the student teachers. The really skinny one, who muttered a lot.

"All right, wake up and pay attention. This is—" Snyder paused, and turned to the young woman beside him. She muttered something which Snyder obviously didn't catch either, and he continued without missing a beat, "—who is going to be monitoring this class while Ms. Ellis is otherwise . . . indisposed."

Buffy jotted her teacher's name in her notebook, with a question mark after it. Anyone upped and disappeared in Sunnydale, it usually bore looking into. Even if the person only ran screaming from the city limits.

"You're to listen to her as you would Ms. Ellis— no, correct that. You're to pretend you are actual students, eager to learn, and listen carefully. Is that understood?"

A faint and ragged chorus of "Yes, Principal Snyder" replied. The small man glared around the room, reserving a particularly venomous stare for Buffy, and then abandoned the student teacher to her fate.

She sat on the edge of the desk, pushed the hair out of her face, and revealed an impishly triangular face with an equally impish grin. And her voice, away from the intimidating nonpresence of the principal, was low but clear.

"Since Principal Snyder neglected to tell me what this class is for, and since I wouldn't trust any of you as far as I could throw you to tell me what you're supposed to be doing here, what say we have a nice, peaceful study hall? You do your homework, and I'll do mine. Deal?"

The "deal" which came back at her was much more enthusiastic than the previous response. *Finally, a student teacher who doesn't seem to have a major bug up her butt!*

73

Thus released, Buffy, Xander, and Willow pulled their chairs together, and returned to their discussion.

"How weird is that?" Xander asked softly, shooting a glance at a student currently skimming through an intimidatingly large-looking textbook. "How could someone know that fast that they want to be a teacher? I mean, weren't they traumatized enough in high school? They didn't even give the wounds time to heal!"

"Yeah," Buffy said. "And then there's college. Assuming any college will take me. Even with decent test scores, it's not like my list of extracurricular activities exactly sparkles. Especially after that incident with the cheerleading team."

"Hey, it's not so bad," Willow said. "We just need to find a school that's looking for people who . . . who have talent but haven't applied themselves yet."

"Gee, thanks, Will. That makes me feel better. What am I supposed to do, look for a college with a high vampire population?"

"Well, you never know. But hey, at least Giles is going to be there with you. Me, though . . ."

"Look, Will, you know college is right for you. And they're going to be falling all over themselves to grab you, from Caltech to MIT, I bet. So no more worrying."

"But . . ."

"But we'll be breaking up the team," Xander said, a little too lightly. "Scattering us all over the states and whatever. So what? Life, you know? And it's not like we won't stay in touch, right?"

"Right," Willow agreed uncertainly.

"Right," Buffy echoed, with forced enthusiasm.

"Right!" Xander repeated firmly. "Hey, what are we getting so heavy for? We're not there yet—and there's lots I want to do before I yell, 'Hey world, here I am!' and the world yells back, 'So what?'"

Buffy and Willow both laughed at that, and Xander grinned.

"All right," Buffy said firmly. "No more moping on stuff that's probably gonna be derailed by the Hellmouth anyway. Deal with the problems we've got right now. Which means getting down to the Case of the Giggling Stranger, and what I'm going to do about it . . ."

"No," Giles said flatly. "Absolutely not. And bring that right foot up higher next time."

Buffy kicked, narrowly missing Giles's chin. "But why? Come on, Giles, it's perfect."

"You don't understand, do you?"

"What I don't understand is why you're being so stubborn. Let's face it, it isn't like you were able to come up with anything better."

A pivot on her left foot brought her into striking range, but Giles got out of the way faster than she had expected. Either she was slowing down, or he was picking up new sneaky moves somewhere, because she hadn't landed a hit on him all session.

"Come on, Giles, why not?" she persisted, coming at him again, but this time leading with the left side of her body, to draw him off.

"Because I don't think that it's a good idea to

bring magic into this. Especially since Willow is not a trained practic—*ooof!*"

Buffy stepped back, feeling rather pleased with herself. He'd gone for her right side, suspecting her left was a feint—and she'd gotten him but good with a sharp left kick to the diaphragm. *Angel was right. Sometimes the most obvious move really is the one to watch out for,* she thought smugly.

"Very nice," he managed to wheeze, taking a step back. "But not enough to incapacitate. Try again."

"No. You're just hoping I'll whup your butt and then feel all happy with myself and stop pushing on this plan. Which is a good plan."

Giles sighed. "No. It is not. It is, in fact, a remarkably bad plan. Believe me," he added grimly, "I have far too much personal knowledge of how easily a novice may bungle a spell." For a second, his face went blank . . . Then he blinked, and the familiar, comfortable Giles was back. "Now. Stand ready, if you will."

Sighing, Buffy fell back into ready mode, balancing evenly and squaring her shoulders as Giles came at her again with the catchpole.

"All right. Then you come up with something better. And . . ." She dodged under his attack with sinewy grace, twirling like she was on the dance floor—". . . you get to explain to Will why she doesn't get to play the Pied Piper of Sunnydale with this thingy. She was going to go out and buy a flute, and everything."

Giles frowned. "I didn't think she played the flute."

"She doesn't."

"Oh." Giles slipped through Buffy's defenses long enough to land a smart thwack across her shoulders. "If you can't carry on a conversation and fight at the same time, might I suggest that you spend a little more effort on the physical?"

No sooner were the words out of his mouth than the Slayer dropped to the floor, her weight supported by her hands while her legs scissored, tumbling him down to the ground in an undignified heap of tweed, the wooden pole falling to the ground above his head.

"You were saying?" she asked, springing to her feet and dusting herself off.

"Yes." He lay there, catching his breath. "Very good. Shall we try again?"

Buffy sighed. *Great. Now he's going to be peeved at Willow for trying to do advanced magic stuff, and take it out on me.*

So much for getting out of practice early today.

The korred snarled, very, very softly. That mysterious Something had been pulling at it all day. An ugly, suggestive pull, deep in its innards.

Someone was working magic on it, from so unfocused and neutral a source that there was no way to locate the magician. The korred had spent the whole day burrowing deeper into the pile of wood and rocks it had found in an empty lot, hiding in its makeshift lair until, with nightfall, the pull faded to the barest of pricklings.

Now, its hunger driving it more than its disquiet,

it had come out of hiding, hunting. But memory of that magic cast over it warned that there was no more time to play. It still was drawn to that one young human girl who glimmered with strength, but it would not be foolish. First it would feed and enhance its own strength. And then—beware, whatever tries to ensnare it. *Beware, glimmering girl.* Beware, everything that gets in its way.

Where would the young humans, the delicious young life forces, be found? It sniffed the air, listened with more-than-human hearing . . . *ah, yes* . . .

The korred stole forward, moving silently from shadow to shadow, avoiding the harsh glare of the lights the humans found necessary, they with their night-blind eyes. It followed the traces that cried *humanity, young humanity* to a human place where the air throbbed and shook with noise. Music, such as had blared from the black box that young human had held.

Wincing, the korred crouched in the shadows, covering its ears, and waited. Eventually, the prey would be found.

But as the night wore on, the korred's temper frayed and at last snapped. Every now and again, the door would open, and young humans enter or exit—but no one came or went from that building alone or even in pairs! It could not hope to snare five, six, *eight* of the creatures!

In a sudden burst of frenzied rage, the korred sank its claws into the earth, tearing up great clumps of grass and dirt. Something surged up from its torn burrow—a mouse, crushed to death in one inhuman hand before it had a chance to squeak. The korred tossed the dead thing from it, then licked the blood from its palm, never taking its glance from that cursed human place.

No! Useless!

Wild with frustration, it raced off into the night. Any human would do now, any human foolish enough to cross its path—*yes!* There was a man, not young, ragged and stinking of hopeless poverty and alcohol. Not much to this life force, but the korred began its song. It saw the man look up and let him see it, knowing that didn't matter. It saw the man's limbs twitch, then lurch into the first clumsy steps.

Yes! the korred thought. *Mine!*

Its song grew louder, stronger. And the man, his eyes widening with dawning horror, began to dance.

CHAPTER 8

Xander finished his breakfast—a Ding Dong and a carton of chocolate milk—and let out a contented little burp. "Breakfast of Champions."

Cordelia made a face at his food choices, but her attention never wavered from the glossy color college brochure she was reading. "I don't know," she said thoughtfully. "I think I've gone beyond the entire Greek experience, don't you? I mean, frat boys are *so* immature." She shook her head, turning the page of the brochure. "On the other hand, once you get out of Sunnydale, maybe they're not all sacrificing to demons, and whatever."

Everyone ignored her, focusing instead on the problem of the moment.

"Well, on the plus side," Willow said with obviously forced brightness, looking up from her laptop's screen, "there haven't been any deaths reported recently." She paused, glancing down at the screen again with a sudden frown. "Just . . . a—a homeless guy got hit by a car. The driver said the guy was just, well, sleeping in the middle of the road."

"But he was alive," Buffy said over her shoulder as she paced. "Well, till the car. What I mean is, it couldn't have anything to do with the korred. Just a really bad drunk."

Willow gave her a hopeful look. "So the korred's still just a maybe-baddie, and not a must-kill-now baddie. Right?"

"Um, yes. So far, anyhow." Buffy swung down into a chair across from Willow, fighting a yawn. "I still need to find a way to get it out of town."

"Before it drives you nuts?"

"Before it gets tired of only stalking and starts to fill its dance card," Buffy said curtly, shadows under her eyes. She had woken in the middle of the night, feeling the weight of someone's blood on her hands. Not an unusual nightmare for the Slayer, who couldn't be everywhere at once no matter how hard she tried. But this nightmare had come with a soundtrack, too. A raw giggle that had almost drowned the screams of the victim.

Almost.

Willow frowned. "What I don't understand is how it's feeding, if it's spending all of its time watching you!"

"Hot dogs, I bet."

Everyone turned to look at Xander, who shrugged.

"Saw a sign up this morning. Missing dog type of sign. Third this month."

Willow's face fell. "Pets are a bad idea in Sunnydale."

"Maybe." But then Buffy realized what she'd said. "About what it's eating, I mean. Not about the pets. I mean—" She gave up. "Giles, what do you—Giles?"

He was rummaging about in the card catalog with the air of a man who's completely forgotten what he's looking for. "How is it," Giles complained over his shoulder as he hunted, "that the addition of a mere half-dozen more students can so disrupt one's schedule?"

"'Cause you're a creature of tweedy habit?" Xander suggested, earning himself a glare from the Watcher.

"Why do you say it that way?" Buffy wondered, distracted for a moment from the weight of worry.

"What?" Giles straightened, turning to look at the little group, his full attention finally caught.

"Schedule." Buffy pronounced it in the British fashion: "Shed-ule. That's so weird. Why do you do that?"

"I, erm, perhaps for the same reason you Americans pronounce it 'sked-jule,' which still sounds rather odd to me. Regional dialect differences, enhanced by extreme—why this sudden interest in linguistics?"

Buffy shrugged. "No real reason. Just enjoying a brief Watcher-Slayer moment. Is that a crime?"

"No." Giles stopped to push his metal-rimmed glasses more firmly up the bridge of his nose. "But it does make one suspicious."

Willow giggled, and Xander marked off a hash mark in the air. "Score one for the Watcher guy."

"Huh. Thanks for that vote of confidence, Giles. You really do know how to make a girl feel wanted, don't you?"

Reassured that her mood was nothing more than the normal snappishness that came of being stalked and not being able—yet—to strike back, Giles returned to his task. "Merely the experience of being your Watcher. Damn. The books I need haven't yet been added to the library's files. Xander, I shall require your assistance this afternoon. There are several boxes of journals in the back storage room that I will need you to bring up."

"Oh, great," Xander groused, resigning himself to an afternoon spent having unfun. "Dust and dusty books. And spiders, I bet."

"Hey, Giles," Willow said, "wasn't cleaning out storage rooms posted as a work-study project in the principal's office?"

Giles blinked, trying to recall the details of what the staff called the "student slave labor" list. "Yes, I believe that it was."

Xander perked up a little at that. "Work-study? As in, pays actual cash?"

"A small stipend, but yes, it does."

"I take it all back. I even take back stuff I haven't said about you yet."

"How . . . gratifying."

"Great," Buffy groused. "Xander, who's already got a job lined up, has yet another cash cow land in his lap. And I'm stuck borrowing and begging." She made a pitiful face at her Watcher. "Can't I do the clean and carry? I could probably do it faster than Xander anyway. And it could double as my workout for the afternoon."

"You have responsibilities already, Buffy." Giles's voice was stern, but his eyes were sympathetic. "First and foremost, to find the korred and remove it as a threat."

She met his gaze, and clear in both their minds was the knowledge that it might already be too late. Buffy could hear Xander and Willow talking about the storage rooms, trying to guess how much junk was back there. And she was aware, all over again, of the fact that no matter how her friends tried to help, no matter how many times they put their lives on the line, they could never really understand what lived in her soul.

She was the Slayer. Giles was the Watcher. And whatever happened in Sunnydale, happened on their watch.

The blood was always on their hands.

"Yeah," Xander said, breaking into her morbid thoughts, "but how're you going to get rid of the Librarian Posse while we do all this loading and hauling?"

"The—?"

Willow giggled, and Buffy rolled her eyes at his

confusion. "The STs, Giles," she translated. "Student teachers. You know—your groupies?"

"Who've latched onto this very room as a prime hanging place?" Xander added, then looked around. "Except when they're all meeting, with the principal. Like now."

Buffy grinned. "And it's not just 'cause they're heavily into books, Giles."

"I—I'm sure you're mistaken."

"No, that's a pretty accurate description," Cordelia said. "Weird, but accurate."

Giles took off his glasses, polishing them with a little more vigor than was really needed. But the edge of his lip curled up in a brief smile before he put his glasses back on and faced them, all seriousness once again.

"Xander!" Cordelia snapped. "Stop that."

"Me? I wasn't doing a thing."

"Just gawking and drooling like some—some freshman, that's all!"

"Hey, I was just imitating the Posse!"

Buffy wasn't listening to them. She was thinking of the korred . . . *What's it up to? Angel knew about it* . . . but Angel wasn't exactly her primary source for information these days. It was too awkward. Too painful. And too dangerous to spend much time with him.

But if he knew about this thing, firsthand knowledge, maybe, then it would be worth getting in touch with him again. Purely for research purposes, of course.

Then she looked up at Giles, and set her jaw. *No. Maybe not.*

"Giles?" Willow said suddenly. "It's going to kill someone, isn't it? The korred, I mean. It's going to escalate, from pets to people."

"Hello? Didn't I say that already?" Cordelia asked, mildly indignant.

"Not necessarily," Giles replied to Willow. "The korred is not quite on the same level as, say, a vampire. It does not require human deaths in order to exist."

Buffy thought he was being just a tad optimistic.

"What, it just kills because it's bored?" Xander asked. "Then here's hoping there's something good on TV every night."

"Not TV," Buffy corrected. "Me. It's stalking me, watching me—I must really fascinate it somehow. So long as I keep doing . . . whatever it is I'm doing, the korred won't cause trouble for anyone else. Right?"

"That, er, is one theory, yes. Although I am not sure that bored is quite the word we were looking for."

Willow nodded. "It's a good theory. I like it. Oh, not that I think it should follow you around all the time, Buffy, I—"

"S'okay, Will. I know what you meant."

"But why?" Xander asked. "I mean, not that the Buffster's not worth following around all night— ow!" Cordelia had given him a slap on the arm.

"I suppose," the Watcher said thoughtfully, "that it may be attracted by her, well, call them 'Slayer qualities.' A supernatural aroma, if you will."

"Are you saying I smell, Giles?"

"But why here?" Xander asked, saving Giles from having to come up with an answer. "Why now? I mean, not that Sunnydale isn't a hopping vacation spot for the undead, but what would bring Laughing Boy out there to us?"

"That, Xander, is an excellent question."

"It is? Do I get extra credit for good questions? Can I maybe make up questions instead of having to give answers? I could get into that."

Giles ignored him. "Why *now*, indeed . . . what could possibly be so special about *now?*"

Willow blinked. "No such thing as korred holidays?"

"Hardly. And there is absolutely no mythic significance about this time of year that would pertain to a creature of its background. No, there has to be something different, something . . ."

"Whoa." Buffy sat straight up. "There is, Giles. I mean, think about it. Who's here who wasn't here before?"

"The student teachers!" Willow gasped.

Giles frowned. "Perhaps." He went into his office, and came out with a small date book. Three of the days were already circled in red, indicating Oz's monthly bouts with wolfiness, but since they were two weeks in the future, he disregarded them. "You say you first became aware of the korred, what, four days ago?"

"Yep."

"And the teachers were here for their orientation on the seventh, which would have been two days before . . . Yes, that could be it. Certainly, a link between the student teachers and the korred is possible; although it is also entirely possible that the timing of the two events may simply be coincidence."

"You know how I feel about coincidences, Giles. Way too often, it's two halves to the same problem. I say we shake one end down and see if an answer to the other half won't fall out."

"An interesting approach" said a sudden, cool, faintly accented voice. "If somewhat . . . undisciplined. Ah yes, here you all are."

Panner stood in the doorway. His cane was gone, but he still looked like he had stepped out of an over-forty edition of *GQ*.

Cordelia perked up at the elegant sight. "Here we are. Who're you?"

"No one with whom you need concern yourself," Giles said so coldly that everyone stared at him. "Yes, Panner? What do you want?"

"Aren't you going to introduce me to your companions? Miss Summers, of course, I have already had the pleasure of meeting. But these must be the others who are aware of who she is. The *Slayerettes*. Interesting."

"You know about . . ." Xander made a wide swinging gesture that could have meant anything from Buffy to the entire history of Sunnydale, and Cordelia ducked out of harm's way as one arm came perilously close to her face.

"Panner is . . . employed by the Council," Giles explained shortly. "Here strictly as an observer, to make notes on our training sessions. Not a common occurrence, but then"—and he cast a warm glance on his Slayer—"Buffy is not exactly common herself."

"Indeed," Panner agreed, making himself comfortable in one of the chairs. "Please. Do go on. I shall be as inconspicuous as a mouse."

"More like a snake," Buffy muttered in Willow's ear. "Slithery, fork-tongued, and all. And we're the mice."

The teens had gone off to their classes, promising to return at the end of the day and continue research—and clearly glad to be out of Panner's sight. Giles had to admit he'd wanted to leave with them. Not so much that he didn't trust Panner. No, it was his own temper that worried him.

But Panner had hung around for only a few minutes longer, making some blatantly false small talk, then had packed up his notebook and tape recorder, and left.

Frustrated? Giles wondered. *Or satisfied that he's played out Round One?*

Alone at last, Giles took advantage of the lull to sit down at his desk with the phone book, and resume his search of the local motels and hotels and bed-and-breakfasts of Sunnydale, trying to ascertain if any of them had a man fitting Ethan Rayne's description staying there.

But, as before, his search turned up nothing.

Which means absolutely nothing when it comes to Ethan, he thought grimly. The man was an adept at the art of not showing up officially. But perhaps, just this once, he was content with the suggestion of interference, and not the actual execution of it . . .

And pigs have sprouted wings. No, Ethan had a reason for calling. And whatever he has in mind, it does not bode well for us . . .

There was nothing more to be done until Ethan contacted him again—or, Giles thought darkly, until something occurred which he could pin on the other man, preferably with a sharp-edged instrument. Returning the phone book to the drawer of the main desk, Giles resumed his more mundane duties as Sunnydale High's librarian, reshelving the few books which had been returned that week. He "tsked" in dismay at the sight of a copy of *The Deerslayer.*

"I don't think the spine on this one has ever been cracked open." Obviously, James Fenimore Cooper had been on some teacher's reading list, based on the number of similar American titles which had been checked out recently. "If they would only inform me of what they plan to assign," he muttered, "life would be a great deal simpler."

A muffled giggle behind him made him spin around, reaching automatically for a nonexistent stake just in case this was the korred.

Instead, it was two of the student teachers.

"Sorry," the shorter of them said. Elaine, her name was, he remembered after a blank moment. She gave him a rather dazzling smile. "We just wanted to know if you had gotten in the *Los Angeles Times* yet?"

"Um, yes. It is over there, on the table with the other newspapers. I haven't had a chance to sort through them yet."

"Thanks." She grinned at him, then, tugging on the arm of her companion—*who can keep track of them all?*—went off to hunt through the pile of newsprint.

Reminded of Cordelia's comment, and Buffy's opinions about coincidences, Giles picked up several books which conveniently needed to be reshelved in that area, and carried them over by hand, rather than moving the entire noisy cart.

"How're you sleeping now?" he overheard Elaine ask the other ST. "Any better?"

"Oh yeah. Much. I must have konked out the minute I hit the pillow last night."

"That's good."

"Yeah. If I didn't get some sleep soon, I was going to start looking like the Teacher of the Living Dead."

Giles started, then realized she was speaking metaphorically. *I have definitely been living on the Hellmouth for too long.*

Satisfied that theirs was merely harmless chatter, he tuned out on the rest of the conversation, only to stop so suddenly he nearly dropped two copies of *The Last of the Mohicans*.

Stalker? Did she just say—

The other one . . . *Sheila, was that her name?* . . . was shaking her head, laughing. "Nope, not a thing since I hit town. It must just have been nerves from driving down here alone. You know, some of those old towns can get pretty creepy when you're alone at night. I probably just got the heebies, and it translated into paranoia. See? That abnormal-psych course was good for something! I can analyze myself."

"Sheil, look, maybe you ought to take it seriously," Elaine said earnestly. "Even if you think he's gone. I mean, you hear about stalkers, crazy guys—maybe you should call the cops or something."

"But I haven't seen anything!" Sheila insisted. "Besides, that's what I was telling you. Whoever he was—if he even was—he's gone now. Nobody creeping outside my window. Unless you count that really creepy senior, the one who wants to take me home to meet his mother. Ugh. Seriously Norman Bates material, you know what I mean?"

"That's cold. True, but cold. But he probably couldn't be any worse than your last couple of dates . . ."

The young women's talk was clearly wandering off in far less useful directions. But Giles had heard enough.

"Oh goodie," Willow chirped, when Giles finally tracked her down between periods, coming out of the computer lab. "Spy stuff. I'm good at that. Nobody ever notices me." She paused, frowning. "That's not a good thing, is it?"

"For the moment," Giles assured her, "it is a very useful thing. For obvious reasons, I cannot very well follow this girl about, or investigate her too closely. And for much the same reason, Xander—"

"No. No letting Xander get anywhere near her.

Any of them. He's got enough trouble with the girls he already knows."

"And Buffy will be occupied with her own obligations. So I'm afraid I must ask this of you. We need to know as much about the young woman as possible: where she is staying, who she associates with, what her background is. Checking up on her family history would not be amiss, either."

Willow nodded, storing all his instructions in her impressive memory. "Okay, so there's a job for Hacker Girl, too. Um, how far—"

Giles held up a hand, a small part of him wincing at the words he was about to say. "Should this search go beyond the established legal parameters—"

"If you didn't know, you couldn't stop me. If I don't tell you later, you can't yell at me. Right."

He did wince then, mostly at the look of anticipation on her face. *You're encouraging her to break the law, for God's sake.*

But there was no help for it. If they were to have any hope of getting rid of the korred, they needed to know what had brought the creature here. If this girl was the key, they needed to know everything they could. One way or another, they *were* going to stop it.

Hopefully, before it stopped one of them.

CHAPTER 9

Midnight. Not a sound other than her own soft footsteps against the cemetery's gravel paths. And yet Buffy knew that she wasn't alone. Just as she knew that it wasn't a vamp watching her.

Geez. This has been going on for . . . how long? Too long, anyhow. I wish the critter would come out of hiding just once. Her hand closed more tightly about Mr. Pointy. *Just for a few seconds. Just long enough. Maybe you can't make a korred go to dust like a vamp—at least Giles says not—but at least I can make it really,* really *sorry it picked me to follow.*

The faintest of giggles sounded behind her—but when Buffy whirled, she saw . . . nothing. Again.

"I'm going to get you," she promised it. "Sooner or later, I'm going to get you."

Yeah. Right. And the Battle of the Bands was going to end in a Disney medley.

"Buffy?"

This time, the recognition—*familiar voice, belongs to Watcher, do not stake*—took over before she could do more than yelp and whirl. The stake flipped in her palm, pointed end away from the newcomer, and she struggled to get her breathing back under control.

"You people have got to stop sneaking up on me like that. Don't any of you watch horror movies?"

Giles tugged at the scarf thing around his neck, then shoved his hands into his jacket pockets. She could never figure out how someone from England could ever be cold in California. Maybe a Hellmouth thing?

"I should not have been able to, as you say, sneak up on you. If *I* could do so—"

"Then so could a vampire, yeah I know. Sorry, I'm a little distracted tonight."

"The korred?" Giles dropped his lecture in favor of more interesting news. He shortened his longer stride to hers as they walked on through the cemetery, and gestured for her to continue.

"Yeah. I think I even saw its eyes glowing, back in the bushes over by the fence. Weird. It's been staying just a couple of—hey!"

"What?" They both stopped, Giles looking alarmed.

"It's gone. I mean, the creepy feeling on the back of my neck . . ." She turned, staring intently into the night behind her. "Yeah. It's gone. Guess Watchers aren't as much fun to stalk."

"Perhaps. I admit, I had hoped that it would

become bored, and wander off on its own by now. Its arrival, this close to the Battle of the Bands, worries me."

"How come? Hey, if it takes out some of those bands—"

She stopped as he gave her the usual glare. "Okay, right. Bad idea. But it's not like anyone would miss some of them."

"While I'm pleased to hear that you're finally beginning to develop some musical discrimination, having the korred in the same vicinity as that large a festive gathering could become rather . . . unpleasant."

"Why? I mean, if it likes to make people dance, then wouldn't that be a really good time to catch it? Because it'll know they're already in the mood to dance, and if we're there, it'll come right to us." Buffy made a motion with her hands, which Giles took to indicate something being wrapped up to her satisfaction.

"We might capture it, yes. Or it might feed off those already gathered before we could stop it. I would prefer to avoid that particular risk if possible."

"Oh. Right." More powerful korred, plus unpleasantly dead teens. "Second rule, do not offer monster a smorgasbord."

They walked in silence for a few more moments.

"Giles?"

"Hmmm?"

She thought for a moment about telling him that Angel had stopped by the other night for a little

Cryptic Guy chat, but decided almost immediately that was a definite Not. It fell into the category of too much hassle for too little usable news. Instead, she brought up the concern that had been chewing at the back of her brain all night.

"Since the first night the korred showed up, the vamps have been playing least-seen. And the few out are newbies, practically falling on my stake. Do you think . . . That's not normal, is it? I mean, as normal as it gets around here, anyway. Do you think maybe the vampires are scared of this thing?"

Giles shook his head. "That seemes unlikely. The korred is an earth creature, a purely natural supernatural creature, if you will. A demon should have no reason to fear it."

"Oh. Just a thought."

"And a good one," he reassured her. She perked up. It wasn't often her thoughts got complimented. "But perhaps, if there has been no demonic activity, you should go home now, and get some sleep?"

"Don't have to tell me twice."

It hissed to itself, stirring restlessly this way, that, pacing in looping circles and getting nowhere. Someone was summoning it, using magic to try and bend it to their will. An annoyance, nothing more, like an itch that could never be scratched, yet wasn't strong enough to harm—the korred snarled, then froze, willing itself to breathe slowly, fade into the shrubbery around it as the danger passed.

In its frustrated rage, it had become careless, had come too close again, so foolishly close—the fearless human girl had almost seen it. That silly wooden spike couldn't kill it, of course, but it was not ready yet for a final confrontation!

Besides, the creature thought, a little more calmly, *someone with so much intriguing power as that young human must never be slain like a mere meal.*

Picking up the track again, it followed at a more cautious distance, learning all it could of its prey.

But the female was no longer alone. An adult male human had joined her, dimming her glow with his mere presence. Frustrated, the korred snarled anew. Magic in that one, muted, so muted. Was he the one who had cast that annoying itch of a spell?

No matter, no matter. The korred could wait. It had not survived all the long ages by rushing unknown prey.

Besides, even if the man hadn't borne that strange glimmer of magic, he was simply too old to provide the proper . . . enjoyment. Younger life forces, the korred knew from its long experience and the more recent . . . mischance, were always far richer, far sweeter.

Ah yes, and since a younger human usually possessed greater endurance as well, the act of taking was always far, far more entertaining. More . . . satisfying.

A thin dark tongue swept across sharp little teeth and it shuddered, feeling hunger blazing through it, hunger roused by the magic itch and not yet appeased.

More strength would be needed to take this young one. Strength it would find from easier sources.

Slipping through the darkness, the korred stole off to begin a new hunt, once more following the hints of *young humanity* to the place where the air was heavy with that harsh, loud music. Settling down behind a bush, it curled up with the patience of a predator. This time, surely, there would be prey . . .

There was. The korred uncurled suddenly with a soundless hiss of pleasure, staring. *Ah yes, yes, at last!* This was a young human male . . . older than those still within the human place by a few mortal years, but still young enough . . . As the korred watched, he saw the young one leave the human place as though thrust out, stammering out broken oaths as he staggered away.

The korred followed. The human's path was erratic at best, and sometimes he cursed, then giggled. And once he stopped to stare at the sky. Just stare. The korred looked up, too, puzzled, but saw only the faint glow of an ugly, hazed sky.

But humans were never predictable. Which was one reason they made such delicious prey. The korred's lips drew back from its teeth in a grin. And it began its song.

To its amazement, the human didn't even try to resist. Instead, eyes wide and wild with what could almost have been . . . awe, he began to dance. Head thrown back, he twisted and leaped and pranced about, and the korred, bewildered by this—this willing sacrifice, began to feed . . .

But something wasn't right. The glow was odd, too bright in places, dimmed in others. The korred shook its heavy head, sweat matting its heavy hair.

Strange, strange, the world exploding in color-light. *Funny trees, funny no . . . terrifying dark, dark. Not warm-dark like a cave, but cold-dark, cold-dark like ice in the vein, ice in the brain—*

The korred broke off its taking, staggering away. The sky whirling in broken shards around it, the korred dove into the bushes and began to burrow as though to escape the madness that clogged its senses.

It never even noticed its victim continuing to dance behind it, the human finally crying out in pain, curling in on himself, and falling to the ground.

CHAPTER 10

Sunnydale High School, home of the Razorbacks, a monument to higher learning and social education. Starting point of young people headed toward a bright future, so forth, so on, so yawn.

Buffy winced. Sunnydale High School, place of noise, was more like it!

To her left, echoing out from an open window somewhere, a really shaky singer was doing his or her best to be heard over a really clumsy bass line. To Buffy's right, echoing from who knew where, some drummer wannabe was working on the same riff over and over—and getting the beat wrong every time.

No doubt about it. The Battle of the Bands was rapidly escalating into a war. And she was just itching to get in there and play UN Peacekeeper.

Maybe start by putting that drum kit over the doofus's head . . .

"Remember, Buffy. Violence isn't always the answer."

Buffy turned to Xander in surprise. "You reading my mind?"

Xander grinned. "No need. It was all over your face. That wonderful I'm-going-to-kick-something-through-a-wall expression we all know and love. And fear."

"Okay. Point taken. Sorry. I'm kinda missing on the sleep thing this week; it makes me irritable."

"Buffy! Wait!" Willow came scurrying up, struggling to catch her breath. "Did you hear the news? I mean, about the college guy?"

"Yeah," Xander said. "Just what we need: an idiot on a drug trip has a heart attack near the Bronze—Snyder's gonna love that, even if the guy wasn't from Sunnydale High."

"A heart attack," Buffy said uneasily.

Willow had her facts down cold. "He's still alive, but the official report said his system was already so screwed up with drugs that he was a—a 'heart attack waiting to happen.' So it couldn't have been the korred, right?"

"Right. I guess." The noise from the bands was growing louder. And more painful. That stupid drummer had gone off the beat—again. And the singer was yowling worse than Oz on a bad moon.

"Let's go find Giles before I hurt someone."

It was quieter in the library—but only a little less

crowded. The Invasion of the Student Teachers continued in full force. All six of the Librarian Posse were already settled in the library, somehow managing to take up all the free work space with their books and papers.

"Lesson plans," Elaine explained over the chatter and rustling of papers, giving Buffy a We're-not-at-all-sorry-for-the-inconvenience smile. "Have to get them organized. You know."

"Yeah. Whatever."

"And they 'simply must' take over the whole library while they do it," Giles murmured to Buffy as he passed.

"Giles, we can't even talk in here! Not with Them here. And outside, well . . ."

"I know," he said dryly. "I'm not going to start a lecture about modern music, or young people who've never even heard of The Who."

"The what?" Xander asked, intentionally picking up on the straight line.

"Exactly. You might want to consider leaving campus for lunch. Your digestion will certainly benefit. We can reconvene in my apartment this evening, where I have most of the books we'll need, just for the duration of this . . . invasion."

"That's 'meet in Giles's apartment for now,'" Willow translated for Xander.

"Hey, I got that!" he said, insulted.

Behind them, the Librarian Posse continued their chatter, Giles looked like he was about to lose his unflappableness, and Buffy and the Slayerettes fled.

* * *

It had been a very long day. And his real work was only just beginning. Rupert Giles felt a twinge in his lower back that had nothing to do with the groceries he was loading into his car. Wincing, he straightened slowly—and then a vaguely familiar silhouette at the corner of his vision caught his attention. He put the last bag into the boot of the car, and closed the lid, staring after the figure, which was rapidly walking away.

No. He had checked every single motel, hotel, and fleabag dumpster in town, to no avail. Ethan had to have more of a self-preservation instinct than to taunt Giles and stay within reach . . .

Then again, the bastard does thrive on being unpredictable.

Dropping the keys in his pocket, the Englishman strode after the now-vanished form, his long legs eating up ground. Any second now . . .

Aha! Turning a corner, he reached out and grabbed his quarry by the shoulder, spinning him around.

"Rupert!" Ethan Rayne gave him a patently insincere smile. "What a delightful surprise. I was just on my way to see you."

"You're beginning to show signs of a death wish, Ethan."

His former friend's face showed nothing but wounded innocence as he tried to free himself from the Watcher's grasp. "Now, now, Rupert. I'm just passing through, thought that I would stop by and give my regards . . . How *are* your young charges these days?"

"Don't start with me, Ethan. I'm in no mood for your little games." *Not now, not ever again.*

"Yes. I know. Simon-pure, our Ripper these days."

"I repeat what I said about a death wish."

Ethan's smile narrowed. "Some new trouble in town, is there?"

Giles felt himself tense in sudden, tightly wound anger. How dare this—

No! He is trying to anger you. He always does. Don't play his childish game.

Forcing himself to relax with an effort, Giles asked coolly, "What do you know about that, Ethan? Is it, perhaps, your doing?"

The other man shook his head sorrowfully. "Coal to Newcastle, my dear Ripper. Your delightful little town is more than capable of creating its own chaos. Not that I don't admire its totally random style . . . Have you ever thought of fumigating?"

Giles's fingers tightened on the other man's shirt, pulling him closer. "I swear to you, Ethan, if I discover that you have had anything to do with anyone in this town getting so much as a hang-nail—"

"Careful, Rupert. You don't want to make a scene in public now, do you? Very bad form for a high school librarian."

Unfortunately, Ethan was right. Much as he wanted to shake the truth from the man, Giles forced himself to release Ethan and back off.

"Much better!" Ethan said, straightening his jacket. "And it's not as if you have any proof of wrongdoing, is it?"

No, it was not. Giles might have his suspicions, but there was absolutely no way to pin the recent occurrences on his old chum—much as he would like to do so. "Go away, Ethan."

With a wicked smile, Ethan went. Giles stood where he was, watching, then at last turned back to his car.

Wonderful. A korred, the Council, and now Ethan. I would almost have preferred another mass vampiric uprising.

Willow settled herself on the sofa in Giles's living room, legs curling under her.

"Okay," she said, consulting her laptop. "You were right, Giles. Sheila Humphries. She's the one who knew what a unicorn horn looked like, even if she said it wasn't one, which it was."

"Unicorn?" Giles had that look on his face, the one he got whenever a new piece of weirdness presented itself to him. Buffy headed that tangent off at the pass.

"Sorry, Giles, no time for unicorn hunts. Long story, short of which is this Sheila chick knows way more about supernatural stuff than she should. Which gives me a bad case of the suspicious."

"Yes," Giles agreed, "that might very well lift her to the top of our list of suspects."

"Anyhow," Willow continued, "she does have this really weird family history. Which would explain her knowing stuff like that. And how she was able to call the korred to her."

"We don't know for a fact that she called the korred, Will. I mean, Giles said she sounded kinda freaked about being followed, right?" Buffy glanced at her Watcher for confirmation.

"It didn't sound as though it were anything she had consciously done, no," Giles said, balancing two heavy books in one hand as he flipped the pages of another.

"So maybe she didn't do it on purpose," Willow continued. "She's still number one suspect, right? According to records, and some really neat genealogical folklore stuff I found, she even had an ancestor who was stoned to death as a witch!" Willow shuddered. "Wow. That must have . . . hurt. They . . . don't do that anymore, do they?"

"Relax, Willow," Buffy said. "They don't. Um, do they?" she added to Giles.

He glanced sharply up from his reference books. "What? Oh, no, no they do not. Not in America. Not legally, at any rate. I believe that the preferred method is—" He looked at Willow's face and stopped short. "Well, never mind. Not germane to the point, is it?"

"Hey, Giles, do you have any, like, diet sodas in here?" Cordelia asked, appearing in the cutaway space between the living room and what passed for a kitchen in Giles's apartment.

"I'm sorry," Giles said somberly. "I failed to stock my refrigerator according to your dietary needs, Cordelia. Next time, I assure you, I will do better."

"Next time? How much longer are we going to be in exile?" she said in dismay, coming back out to join the others, empty-handed. "I mean, okay, the library is geeky enough, but—What?" she asked when Xander tried to muffle her with a hand over her mouth. "What?"

"Sorry," he said to the others. "She has these fits, words come out of her mouth, the new medication was supposed to take care of that."

"Please, Willow," Giles said, ignoring Cordelia's struggle to free herself, "go on. You were saying?"

"Well. There's kind of a pattern here. It doesn't look like Sheila is any sort of, you know, psychic. Or at least not one who knows she's got any sort of abilities. But she does come from a family with genuine talent. I . . . guess."

"You guess," Buffy echoed.

Willow hesitated, scrolling through the files. "I mean, there's evidence they really *were,* uh, for real. But they don't seem to have been too reputable. I mean, they even got thrown out of . . ." She looked up from the screen, wide-eyed. "They got thrown out of Cornwall. That was over a hundred years ago, though."

Buffy straightened. "Okay. Cornwall. That's where the korred's from, too, right? So, connection. Way too freaky, and may I say again I do *not* like coincidence.

"So say Sheila really does have a psychic whatever, even if she doesn't know it. And she smells kinda like home, maybe. So maybe the korred got curious and started following her."

"Yes . . .," Giles mused. "That is quite plausible. The korred followed her to Sunnydale, drawn by the scent of ability . . . and then got, er, sidetracked by your more powerful scent."

"You keep saying that, Giles. Should I be, like, showering with some kind of antiweirdness deodorant soap, or something?"

"I'm afraid that it isn't that simple." His tone was a combination of amusement and exasperation.

"Is it ever? Okay, don't answer that. So Sheila brought it to us, not knowing, and then it changed its little stalker mind, decided I felt tastier. Great. Any ideas yet how to catch a korred? Or chase it away before anyone gets killed?"

"Hopefully. Willow, if you would do the honors for the Internet, I will see if I can't find something in my books about how to lure a korred away from its chosen hunting ground. Xander, you and Cordelia will need to watch for any more missing animal reports."

"Yeah," Buffy cut in, "and see if maybe we can track the korred's trail that way."

"Excellent!" Giles said. "See if the missing animal reports do provide a trail. But don't try to catch the korred on your own!"

"Hey, no problem!" Xander agreed. "Not catching monsters is what I excel at."

"Yes, and check the newspapers, to make sure that we haven't been missing any failed attacks on humans." Giles shook his head. "I never thought I would be thankful for that ghoulish practice of listing the police blotter in the newspapers . . ."

"And I get to . . . stand around looking Slayerish again," Buffy added. "Nice not to have to learn any new lines, no matter what the play." Buffy polished her nails against the fabric of her top, and sighed dramatically.

"You will be needed later," Giles assured her. Buffy saw the look in his eyes, and swallowed hard. *He thinks we'll be hearing about victims soon. Dead-type victims. And not the animal kind, either.*

"Giles," she murmured, "the college kid with the heart attack. And before, the homeless guy, the one the car hit. You don't think they're, well . . ."

"Failed korred attacks? I don't know. There is a perfectly mundane explanation for both incidents. But," he added, glancing down his glasses at her, "I like coincidence no more than do you."

Why does it always come down to this? Why can't we ever catch the bad things and put them away before they hurt anyone? Why is it always . . .

Why, why why. Stop asking why, Buffy. Because, that's why.

"And to go for snacks now," Xander was saying. "Speaking of which, no offense to the offered munchies, Giles, but I'm feeling the severe need for pizza."

A loud grumble, from the vicinity of Buffy's stomach, seconded that opinion.

"Yes," Giles agreed. "Go. But stay together, all of you. Until this thing is caught, I want the, um, buddy system firmly in place."

"Can do," Xander said, putting one arm around Cordelia, the other across Willow's shoulders. Willow flinched, then slid out from under his grip. Xander continued after only the slightest of pauses, "We'll be joined at the hip. Practically."

"In your dreams, Xander," Cordelia retorted, shrugging off his arm and leading the way out the door.

"Oh, but what about Oz?" Willow said suddenly. "I've got to warn him, 'cause of his being a, well, you know, and all!"

Giles tensed. "Oh dear. Yes, I hadn't thought of that. Ring him up right now and leave a message."

Buffy waited till Willow was on the phone and Xander and Cordelia had gone out the door, then scooted closer to her Watcher, murmuring confidentially, "Giles?"

"Hmmm?" He looked up from clearing away the remainder of their snacks.

"This korred . . . if it's attracted to stuff that's supernatural and whatever . . ." She looked over to where her best friend was obviously speaking to an answering machine. "Is Willow going to be in any danger? I mean, because of her messing around with magic?"

Giles put down the cup of tea he had just picked up, and took off his glasses, contemplating them as though the answer was written there. "I have already considered that."

"And . . . ?" she prompted.

"Buffy, by now you should know there aren't always clear answers to questions, particularly those dealing with the supernatural. But no, I do not believe that she will be in any immediate danger. Not at her current level of involvement. At this point, with so much supernatural activity stirring within the Hellmouth, I believe that the korred is focused on your aura, as the Slayer, to the exclusion of everything else."

"What about you?" Buffy asked. "I mean, you know way more magic than Will, and . . . well, the connection, the whole Watcher thing . . ."

Giles smiled, rather ruefully. "I don't think that I will have that much trouble, unfortunately."

"Huh?"

"From the research I've done, the korred is, um, how to say this—it feeds more strongly off those still growing. More energy is generated by adolescent bodies, you see—"

"What you're saying is, you're too old for it."

"Well. Yes."

"Good." She noted his reaction and backtracked. "I mean . . . fewer people I have to worry about, the better. I'm going to take this thing down, Giles. Somehow. And soon. Because I am getting really, really tired of waiting to get tagged. Someone's got to explain to that annoying little giggler that '90s women do not take kindly to being stalked all across town."

CHAPTER 11

Principal Snyder, of course, had been against "turning a bastion of learning into a commercial venue." That meant, as far as Buffy could tell, that he hated the idea of anyone using his name to have any fun. But he had been overruled for once by the school board, who had decided that anything that brought music—any kind of music—into teenage lives was a good thing. By now, banners advertising the Battle of the Bands had been hung across just about every doorway in Sunnydale High.

Of course, since most of them were crepe paper, they were already beginning to look pretty tacky. As Buffy and Giles walked together, he was nearly trapped in a garish yellow loop of sagging crepe paper. Giles delicately backed out of it without tearing so much as an inch of the banner, and Buffy stifled what would have been a really inappropriate laugh.

Inappropriate basically because of what he'd told her just before walking into the banner.

"So, you think that homeless guy they found maybe had been attacked by the korred, after all?" she asked.

"Perhaps." Dignity recovered, he walked on, Buffy beside him. "Magic takes a great deal of energy, just as athletic activity does, and in order to replace that energy the korred must feed. And the other victim, that unfortunate college student, did mention something about a dance."

"Hey, you didn't tell me that!"

"Er . . . no." Giles glanced sideways at Buffy. "Quite frankly, though, I was surprised that it had been able to hold out this long merely on the occasional squirrel or stray dog."

A flash of irritation shot through her. "But you didn't see fit to share that surprise with me?"

"Would it have sped our research along any faster?"

"No," Buffy had to admit. "We're pretty much moving under urgent, already. But, still! This is no time for you to turn into not-sharing-stuff guy, okay?"

"Agreed. In the future, I will inform you of every anomaly or fluctuation in the otherwise normal practices of the Hellmouth, so that you, too, may earn gray hairs worrying over what they might mean."

"Okay, you're doing the sarcasm thing again. Don't. People will start thinking you have a sense of humor, and then we'll really never get them out of the library."

"What on earth is Willow doing?" Giles asked, stopping in midstride.

Buffy followed his gaze down into the courtyard. Sure enough, there was Willow, accosting students and faculty alike as they walked by, and thrusting pieces of paper in their faces. The look on the redhead's face was a combination of surprised satisfaction when someone took and read the paper, and terrified disbelief that she was actually being so bold.

"True love is a force more powerful than anything else, Giles," Buffy said, summing up the situation in one glance. "Oz must have asked her to hand out flyers for the Battle, to get more warm bodies into the Bronze tonight. With how bad most of our school bands are, a home team advantage would naturally go to the Dingoes."

"Strategy. Very impressive."

"Hey, Oz may be the überslacker sometimes, but he takes the music seriously. Music and Willow. He's a guy with priorities."

Just then, a particularly obnoxious teen tossed the flyer back into Willow's face, and the girl looked as though she had been slapped, both angry and upset at the same time.

"Whoops. Looks like it's time for some positive reinforcement," Buffy said. "With Will, when she gets upset you never know if she's going to bolt, or turn 'em into a frog."

"Frogs," Giles murmured uneasily, following the Slayer down the stairs. "There are no spell books in the library that deal with frogs. Are there?"

"Oh! Hey! Have a flyer. Battle of the Bands tonight at the Bronze. Over half-a-dozen bands will be playing for one low cover fee, including our own Dingoes—"

"Hey. Will. Calm down, it's me. I've already agreed to be cheering squad, remember?"

"Oh." Willow blinked, mentally cycling herself down a few notches. "Sorry. I just blurt and don't think, so it all gets out without me stumbling over anything. Did you see me? I was good, wasn't I? Handing them out, and everything."

Buffy turned to look accusingly at Giles, who shook his head. "I didn't let her anywhere near the caffeine this morning," he said. "Ah, Willow, if you have quite finished your tour of duty as publicity shill . . ."

"Sure. Here."

Before Buffy could react, Willow had shoved the remaining flyers into her hands. Buffy promptly shoved them into the hands of Jonathan, a classmate, who gave her a wild-eyed glance. At her glare, he scurried off. "Job done," Buffy said.

"Ah, yes," Giles cut in hastily. "Willow, I found an anomaly in the police records that might be of interest to us. Apparently a car struck and injured a homeless man two nights ago—a man who staggered into the driver's path as though drunk or deathly ill."

"Uh, Giles," Buffy said, "that isn't exactly news."

"Unfortunately, no. But what is unusual is that, as far as I could tell without having access to the full medical records, the man was neither drunk nor ill, merely . . . weary."

Willow blinked. "Then you do think the korred . . ."

"We can't be sure. Not without more facts. A korred typically kills what it attacks. Of course, it is possible that he escaped, or was released when the korred found his energy lacking in some way. But, Willow—"

"Got it. You want me to get that full medical report on the homeless man and on the drugged college kid, to compare damage done, maybe get a better idea of how the korred works. Computer research. Cool!"

Giles and Buffy exchanged glances. "She scares me sometimes," Buffy said in a confiding tone.

"Well. Ordinarily I would be loathe to encourage you in your more, ah, illicit habits with that machine. But—"

"Giles, you are about to get majorly research geeky, aren't you?"

"—this is an unparalleled opportunity to do field work in an area which has—" Then what Buffy had just said registered. "Yes. Well. That is . . ."

"Never mind!" Willow said brightly. "I'll get right on it."

As she eagerly hurried off, Giles soberly agreed with Buffy, "Terrifying. Now, as to our plan for tonight . . ."

* * *

Buffy reached around the vampire trying to put the big hickey on her, grabbed the scruff of his neck, and pulled him forward over her head. He landed with a reassuringly solid thud on the pavement, and then turned into even more reassuring gray dust when she followed through with a stake to the heart.

"I'd give that one a 7.5," she decided. "Points lost for actually letting him get his grubby paws on me. Which would make tonight's average . . . 27.6. And they said I couldn't handle basic math."

Smiling grimly, she pocketed the stake and checked her watch, then looked around, realizing for the first time that she had come to a part of town that was relatively new to her.

"Lovely. Another tourist must-see location. This would be the perfect place for a crazed psycho killer to jump out at me now," Buffy muttered to herself. "Like in one of those stupid movies. One of those where the guys says, 'Hey, you go check the basement alone.' And the girl's too dumb to carry a flashlight. A working flashlight."

Well . . . she didn't carry one, either. But.

And the fact was, it *was* the kind of spooky, mist-filled night filmmakers love. Prime psycho territory.

"Only psycho killers know better than to come anywhere near Sunnydale. Unless they happen to be psycho killers who are vampires, in which case they're Drusilla. Who is so not my problem anymore."

It was always a bad sign when she started to talk to herself on patrol. At the moment, even Cordelia would have been welcome company. Just a couple of random vampires, too new to give her much of a fight. The severe boredom they were giving her was mixed, though, with a sense that someone, somewhere was laughing its head off at her.

The korred. She'd bet her last dollar on it. *Assuming, that was, that I have a dollar to bet.*

Was that a sound? Buffy whirled—and a wild something roared up in her face! She lunged blindly—

Idiot. Just an owl. Lucky for you.

She'd startled her fellow late-night hunter into taking off in a rush, almost in her face. Once Buffy's heartbeat had gotten back down to normal, she managed a casual shrug and kept going. Another night, another walk, another couple of vamps staked. Just another typical day at the office. At least there still was no sign of the Midnight Giggler actually showing up. Yet.

"Whoa. Activity. And not of the fun sort, either."

Lights up ahead—yeah, her ability to tell flashing-light types apart was coming in handy. That was definitely a police car. Lights flashing, right, but no siren . . . yeah, and that blocky shape was an ambulance next to it, just outside the cemetery gates.

They weren't rushing, which was always a bad sign. But not a vamp attack. She hoped. Had the korred . . . ?

"Should I . . . ?" She stood in the shadows, watching the activity, torn by rare indecision.

"Nope. If it was a vamp attack, there's nothing I

can do now. Giles will know if I need to stake someone before they take up the undead nonlifestyle tomorrow."

Besides, if she went over there, she was going to have to answer some really awkward questions, such as what a teenage girl was doing out wandering in the cemetery alone at night.

"Sorry, whoever you were," Buffy said softly, and went her way.

"Hey," Willow greeted Buffy when they met outside school the next morning. "You look tired. Bad night?"

"There've been better." She shrugged casually, shifting her books to the other arm. "Been lots worse."

"I hear you. I was up almost until midnight, working on a program that's due tomorrow. But it was really interesting—come on, we've got time before class, I'll show you."

"Sure. Why not?" The hacker's computer programs were always good for making her feel like a total knownothing. "Besides, I've got to check in so Giles knows that I made it to school safely."

"Hey." Willow pushed the library doors open, and stopped in shock. "No Librarian Posse. We've got our home back!"

"The day is young," Buffy said, refusing to get her hopes up.

As they took over their usual table before any student teacher could sneak in and steal it from them, Willow flashed Buffy a nervous little grin. "So? How did it go?"

"I don't know. I mean, I saw the cops and an ambulance—"

"Buffy. I meant the test. You know? The math makeup? The one you had to wheedle and beg for?"

"Oh. Not too bad. Who knows? I might even have passed this time."

"Cool!" Willow hesitated a moment, then asked, "But *did* you hear any details about what happened last night? I mean, you must have been pretty close. Did you see anything?"

"Uh, like what? What else?"

"They found a body there, just outside—"

"The cemetery gates. Will, I know that part. Who was it?"

"Some guy with a weird name. Um, Bear-something. Nightbear. Morgan Nightbear. Big guy, ponytail? One of the custodial crew, the one they send up on the ladder to fix windows? I guess he worked part-time for the county, too, 'cause they say he was there repairing a broken door, or something."

The name sounded vaguely familiar. "Geez, wait . . . recent graduate, right? A couple of years ahead of us?"

"That's right. He dropped out of college, came back to town." Willow paused. "Imagine *wanting* to work in a cemetery—oh. I didn't mean—"

"I don't *want* to work there, Will. It just . . . happens. Hey, but he wasn't much older than us! And if he'd just been hired, they would have given him a physical, right?"

"I guess." Her friend tilted her head, clearly wondering where Buffy was going with that thought.

"So it probably wasn't one of our few and far between natural deaths, was it?" Buffy asked with growing dismay. And she hadn't done her sweep of the cemetery last night. Maybe if she had . . .

"Coronary failure," Giles replied from behind them.

Buffy sank back in her chair, weirdly relieved, until the impact of that sank in.

"Oh. You mean . . ."

"Heart attack? He's escalated," Willow said, nodding, her eyes wide.

Xander and Cordelia entered just in time to hear that.

"So, this guy they found last night was danced to death?" Xander asked. "Weird. Even for the Hellmouth, that's weird."

"Gross," Cordelia proclaimed. "So, what happens now?"

Giles pushed his glasses more firmly in place. "Escalate our efforts as well. Um, Buffy, we shall have to up your patrols. I'm afraid that dinner with your mother—"

"Is off the schedule. I can deal with that. Mom'll deal. She's got that whole people-dying-not-good-for-the-digestion thing, anyway."

"Is this your idea of a jest?"

The sudden, faintly accented voice made everyone start.

Giles recovered first. "Panner."

"Of course, Panner." The observer stalked fiercely forward. *Like,* Buffy thought, *an angry teacher.* "What do you think you are doing?" Panner snapped. "Eh? What?"

"We are doing our jobs." Giles bit off the words, eyes cold behind his glasses.

"And do those jobs, Watcher and Slayer both, do those jobs entail such complete and utter *inefficiency?*"

"Hey." Willow's voice wasn't very loud, but it was firm. "That's not fair."

To Buffy's surprise, Panner's angry scowl softened. "The blame doesn't lie with you, child. You cannot be expected to deal with things of this measure."

Willow's face went absolutely blank. Which was, Buffy knew, her very, very polite way of saying, "You just struck out, Mister."

"Go away, Panner." It was almost a growl from Giles. "Let us work."

For what seemed like a long time, neither Giles nor Panner moved. Then Panner shook his head. "So be it." He turned and stalked away. But just as he was passing through the doorway, Panner added over his shoulder, "For now."

Xander was the first to recover. "Geez. Some weird school buds you have, Giles."

"Yes. Indeed. Forget about him for now. Instead, let us sum up the current situation."

"Right." Buffy began ticking off the points on her fingers. "Let's see. There's the korred stalking Sheila, who may or may not have a clue that she's in danger—and may not even be in danger now that it's gotten a whiff of me. So to speak. There's the korred stalking me. There's me stalking vamps, who are being noticeable no-shows this week, and no note for teacher. And, ta-da, me stalking the korred, who definitely isn't playing well with others. Does that about cover it?"

"Someone else may be involved," Giles added reluctantly. "Namely, Ethan Rayne."

Buffy sighed. "Of course. Wouldn't be a party without him."

"That creepy man." Cordelia shuddered dramatically. "What does *he* want?"

"I'm not sure. Knowing Ethan, possibly the korred. Possibly not."

"Oh great!" Xander said. "Just what we needed, another complication. I want one of those pads, the ones with all the colored markers, so we can keep track of who's doing what to who."

"Whom," Giles corrected absently.

"Whatever."

Buffy glanced at the others. "All right, I'll say it. The korred's started feeding. That means it's gonna get stronger. And once it's strong enough . . . it's just a matter of time before the korred gets one of the two of us it's stalking." She shrugged, faking nonchalance. "If it's me, hey, no sweat. I've faced worse. And then that creepy little hairy stalker'll get what's coming to it."

Willow looked from Giles to Buffy. "But what

about Sheila—she's still, you know, vulnerable! It could grab her first."

"Good point," Xander said. "But what can we do about it? I mean, this may be Home of the Weird, but you can't just walk up to someone and say, 'Hey, guess what? You're being stalked by a crazed dance master who's going to suck your—what is it sucking again?'"

"The life force," Giles said patiently. "Your *chi*, if you will. An essence—"

"Right. Who's going to suck out your life force. Although," Xander added thoughtfully, "she *is* kind of pretty. Tell you what: I'm willing to give it a try— *ow!*"

Cordelia looked innocently at the others, shaking her hand to get rid of the impact sting. "What?"

"So," Giles said, "if there is nothing more to be added just now, I shall suggest that you return to your normal lives."

"Hah," Buffy muttered.

"Ah, well, yes. Buffy, I would like a few words with you. If you would."

"Oooh, Buffy's got detention!" Xander chanted. "Buffy's got detention."

He darted out the door just before Buffy could swat him as well, and Cordelia and Willow went with him. Buffy turned to Giles.

"Yes?"

"I, ah, need your help."

"You got it. You know that. Ah, wait." She looked at him, suspicious. "What sort of help?"

"Sheila. If she is unaware of what is happening . . . I must speak to her. But . . . I'm sure you can see why I cannot do it alone."

Buffy paused, thought it over, then burst out laughing. "Giles! You want me to be your chaperon!"

"Well, yes. In a manner of speaking."

She stared at him in delight. "You're blushing!"

He pushed his glasses more firmly up his nose. "I most certainly am not."

"Are too! Don't worry, Giles. I'll make sure the little teacher doesn't hurt you."

"Delighted to hear that," he muttered.

"Hey, just in time. Look who walked in."

"Ah."

He was clearly unsure how to start this, so Buffy shrugged and headed for the group of STs who were settling themselves at the long table. "Sheila, right? Mr. Giles needs to ask you a few questions."

Oh boy, she's got a happy, Buffy thought. *No problem at all steering her into Giles's office. Getting her out, now, that might be a problem . . .*

Buffy perched on the edge of his desk, trying not to knock any books off it, and watched him in action.

"Ms., ah, Humphries. Please, be seated. I'll try not to take too much of your time. This is rather awkward, ah . . . I have a hobby, you see. Historical genealogy. I was, ah, working on a project, and I found references to a Humphries family from Cornwall. Unusual name for a Cornwall family . . . Welsh, I should say, more typically. I was wondering if you might, perhaps, be able to help me, if you knew where your family came from?"

Stodgy but not stupid, Buffy thought. *Way to go, Giles.*

"Well, I think we did come from Wales, way back when, yes. Isn't that funny, you coming across my family!"

"Quite. Funny stories, too. In the peculiar sense."

"Funny? Oh. That. Must be my family then, yeah." The young woman leaned forward to add, more softly, "I'm afraid some of the Humphries weren't all that, you know . . ."

"Honest?" Buffy contributed.

Sheila glared at her. "Things couldn't have been too great back then. You did what you had to."

"Of course," Giles soothed. "But—"

"Look, if you're going to ask me something stupid, like do I believe in that psychic stuff my grandfather peddled . . ."

"You don't believe in such things."

Hey, cool, Giles! You made it sound like you don't, either!

Sheila shrugged. "Only in the movies."

When Giles didn't volunteer anything, she got to her feet. "Well, it's been interesting. Knowing we're in history books, I mean. If you want to know anything more about the family, stuff that's not in the official records, just ask. Although I'm not sure it'll be much help to your project."

"My project. Ah, yes. I will," Giles assured her solemnly. "Thank you." But as she was leaving, he added, very casually, "Oh, I might add . . . I couldn't help but overhear something you were saying about being followed."

"Oh, that! Just some stupid kid. I mean, giggling? Come on!" But her voice wasn't as steady as it might have been.

"Of course," Giles said, soothingly. "And it's true that Sunnydale is a low-crime town."

As Buffy nearly strangled, choking down a laugh, Giles added, "Still, these *are* modern times. I really do doubt that you're in any danger. But it certainly couldn't do any harm for you to take the normal precautions that a young woman has to take these days, especially if you must be out after dark."

"Can't be too careful when you're out after dark," Buffy agreed cheerfully. "I know I always am. Got a stake in my survival."

So to speak.

CHAPTER 12

It shivered, giggled, licked its leathery lips with delight, tasting the glow still lingering in the air around it. Oh, what fun that had been, what wonderful fun! The prey had been young and healthy, aura sparkling and shimmering in the air, full of strength. And he had danced so well, for such a long, long while, fighting the pull of its magic before falling to his knees. *And right in the cemetery!*

Young ones had so much power in them, so much vitality. When it had forced the human back to his feet, he had gone on and on for a delightfully long time again, allowing it to suck the vigor off its healthy core. But not even the best prey lasted. Shaking, shuddering, limbs limp and eyes wild and helpless, the human had at last fallen and writhed and then, ending the fun, lain still. It had drunk down the last fleeing life force then, the marrow stuff so delicious, so exciting—*ah, yes!*

It had waited too long for such as this, enticed as it had been by the young female hunter. Too long, and it had suffered for it. Not been strong, not been swift as it could be. Now it felt that human's strength flow through it, the stolen vigor making the night air itself sparkle around it.

But one full dance, one death, one drinking of rich young life force had not been enough. *There must be more dancing, more feeding!*

It would wait no longer.

"You know," Xander said suddenly, looking up from the ancient book lying open on Giles's coffee table, "it can't be healthy for us to spend so much time in school. All those florescent lights, they can't be good for us. And I bet studying so much outside of school isn't good for us, either. All that lack of fresh air and exercise, you know? Rots the brain or something."

"Xander . . ."

"Hey, I'm looking, I'm looking." He turned another page, coughing a little as dust rose off it. "Man, these books are so stuffy even Giles can't read them."

"Thank you *so* much, Xander," Giles commented from his own pile of books. "Less a case of stuffiness, and more the fact that a korred is not exactly a common phenomena, particularly not in North America. It is a creature of the earth—as in the four primal elements, not the periodic chart."

That got blank looks from Buffy, Xander, and Cordelia.

"Earth, air, fire, and water," Willow contributed helpfully. "Uh, not literally. I mean, there's still sodium and iron and all those other things—"

"Four symbolic elements," Giles continued before she could get lost in her sentence. "The korred, as a creature of earth, is a manifestation of magic evolving into a physical form. Therefore, it is not a demon or otherwise truly extradimensional, and as such would generally not be unduly influenced by the Hellmouth."

Xander and Buffy both looked at Willow for translation.

"He didn't see any need to unpack these books until now," she said.

"Oh. Why didn't he just say that?"

Willow closed the oversized journal she was reading, and pushed it across the table to the "not helpful" pile, then reached for another, much smaller journal. It was one of those leather-bound notebooks, the kind without lines on the paper, that they sold as diaries and such for people who had really deep thoughts—or thought that they did, anyway. Way newer than everything else they'd been reading . . .

Flipping open the cover to a random page, Willow stopped, recognizing the cursive scrawl.

"Giles? Um, I think this one's yours . . ."

He came over to the table, taking the journal from her outstretched hands. "Good heavens. So it is. From my days at university." He looked about at the others, explaining, "I suppose I packed this along with all the others, placing it by subject rather than by importance or antiquity."

Xander shrugged. "I dunno, from when you were in college? That's gotta be antique-land by now."

"I think I still have a few years to go before I qualify as an antique," Giles said dryly.

"But this does have stuff about korreds in it?" Willow asked impatiently. "Or at least, earth magic things?" Her eyes were practically glowing as she took the book back from him.

"Well. Yes. I took a course on ancient and contemporary agriculture-based mythologies. It was a requirement, although I had, of course, been studying that sort of thing for many years before. I, ah, I'm afraid I slept through most of it."

"A gut course," Xander said, nodding. "G-man, I'm impressed!"

"So nice to know that something in my life meets with your approval." His lack of being impressed seemed lost on Xander, who shrugged and reached for another Dorito.

Buffy looked over Willow's shoulder, just skimming the words on the page. "You took good notes for a sleeping person," she noted. "I've got to learn me that trick."

Willow began turning pages rapidly, searching for a particular word to jump out at her. "No, no . . . this is why books should come with a find-and-replace key . . . here we go! Korreds." She paused, squinting at the page, then handed the book back to

Giles. "Um, your handwriting kinda squiggles here."

"Right." He unfolded his glasses and fit them back onto his nose; *almost,* Buffy thought, *as though he was making a ceremony out of it.* Then he began to read out loud.

"'Korred. Also known as crion, jetin, kourican, and related names.'"

"Lot of aliases for one critter," Xander noted.

"'Cause a lot of different people know about it, I bet," Buffy said, and Giles gave her a glance of approval.

"Exactly. Not a very useful fact, though, I'm afraid." Giles read on, "'The korred is also said to be closely related to the spriggan.' Again, interesting, but not precisely helpful." He was silent a moment more, glancing down one page, then another. "Oh dear."

Buffy tensed. "What?"

"I quote, 'Korreds, not being demons, can't really be dispelled or banished in a timely fashion.' Now, don't look so worried. I suppose my note merely meant that normal spells of demonic banishment won't work. But here, I did go into a bit of korred lifestyle, as it were . . . solitary, for the most part—"

"Good. One is one too many already," Cordelia said.

"They are not averse to sharing their locale with humans, but it seems that they prefer to live below sea level, in caves or even bogs."

"Well, that narrows it down!" Buffy said in disgust. "I mean, Sunnydale's not exactly on a mountain or anything. And the whole place is full of underground tunnels and shafts."

"Which tend to be filled with vampires." Xander pretended to be marking off a list. "Scratch tracking the critter to its lair."

"Wait, wait," Willow cried. "Here's a story about a korred . . . oh." She looked up in dismay. "It's not a very nice one. Seems a mother thought that a korred had stolen her baby and left a fake one in its place. A—a changeling, you know? And so she . . . beat the baby to make it confess—"

"Never mind that," Giles cut in kindly. "That's merely fiction, a misunderstood fairy legend someone mixed up with stories about korreds." He glanced at the others. "There are several more books to examine. And no moaning in self-pity, either. Xander, if you wish to go on to college, you really must learn how to do proper research."

"Who says I want to go on to college?"

"'Do you want fries with that?'" Buffy muttered under her breath.

Giles looked about the room. Books were piled on just about every flat surface. The sun was barely filtering through the window, indicating how late it had gotten. "Well. I, ah, think it's safe to say that we have investigated every available source."

"And not gotten anywhere," Buffy complained.

"Not quite. Granted, all the books are remarkably

silent on the matter of getting rid of these creatures. But that hardly means there isn't a way."

Xander stretched. "All right, korred. This here town's not big enough for the two of us."

"Yeah, right," Buffy said. "Gunfight at the Sunny-dale Corral. No thanks. The cowboy look is so gone it's already had its comeback and died again. No, I just want this thing out of town, and I want it as easy as possible . . . Hey, Giles? What about somehow tricking it into leaving town?"

"Or . . ." he added, "perhaps we could entice it to someplace more appealing. Willow, if you would kindly return my journal . . . ? Willow!"

She looked up, startled. "I was just studying—"

"Precisely what worries me. Lord only knows what I wrote in the margins."

With a sigh, Willow surrendered the journal. Giles riffled quickly through it, as though trying to see if she'd managed to remove any pages, then continued, "According to my notes, korreds are attracted to rocks and minerals. And I would guess that the odds are fairly high that the town Sheila passed through, when she first attracted the korred's attention, was an old mining town."

"That's right!" Willow said. "There are lots of those to the north of here. I saw a documentary once," she added to Buffy.

"Exactly," Giles cut in. "So, if we could just lure it back there, to where its long-term home is . . . As-suming, of course, that we could discourage its fascination with you, Buffy."

"So I guess 'Shoo! Go away!' won't work, huh?" Xander asked.

The others ignored him.

"The only other answer, really," Giles said, "is to kill it. But, unfortunately, the books are silent on how that is to be done as well."

Buffy shrugged. "And I bet that staking it isn't going to do the same 'poof, you're dust' it does on vampires."

"No."

She leaned over Giles's arm to look at the woodcut illustration. "Yeah, and that hide looks thick enough to deflect anything short of a missile launcher."

Xander perked up. But before he could do more than open his mouth, Giles stopped him with a stern look and a "Definitely not."

"But—"

"There were too many, ah, civilians about the last time that you tried that trick. I do not want to risk more lives and awkward questions if there's any other option."

"Besides," Buffy said. "I really don't want to get stopped by the cops with a launcher strapped to my back. Getting expelled once was bad enough— there's no need to let that troll Snyder do a happy-feet dance on my life again."

Willow frowned. "How does the korred do it? I mean, get its victims to dance themselves to death?"

"That's a very good question, Willow," Giles said. "Actually, I'm not sure. But legend has it that it emits some manner of high-pitched music that takes control of the human body."

"So," Willow said reasonably, "all you have to do is not listen, right?"

"It's not quite that simple . . ." Giles began to say, then stopped. "Or . . . perhaps it is!"

"The Oddy-something!" Buffy cried. "You know, that old book they made into a movie?"

"Ah, the wonders of a modern education. *The Odyssey,* indeed."

"Well, there was something in it, you know. The hero wanted to hear those singers, but it was too dangerous because they, like, lured people to them. And ate them, or something. So he . . ."

"Precisely," Giles said. "It *is* dangerous, though."

Buffy shrugged. "Hey, you know what they always say in the movies: 'Danger' is my middle name!"

"Yes, well, too often 'In' is their first name," Giles retorted, and went to get himself more tea before anyone could reply.

CHAPTER 13

"I could learn to hate this town," Ethan Rayne muttered, a little out of breath. *No, more than a little. And, curse it all, this jacket was never going to be the same.*

He glanced warily over his shoulder . . .

Blast! There they were again, no less than four really ugly, really angry-looking vampires. Construction workers in life, judging from the muscling still on them and the way one of them had nearly torn the sleeve off Ethan's jacket. Easily as a child ripping tissue wrapping off a present.

With a shudder, Ethan ducked out of the alley, onto Sunnydale's main street for perhaps five seconds, then just as quickly darted into another alley, swearing silently all the while. It wasn't as though he'd actually been up to anything reprehensible! No, he had been minding his own business, doing nothing more terrible than trying to track down the mysterious creature he had discovered in this forsaken town. *Nothing wrong with that, surely? Simple curiosity, and all that?*

Curiosity killed the cat, Ethan reminded himself, then snorted. *Must have been a singularly stupid feline.*

Unfortunately, while he'd been investigating, he had surprised, and been surprised by, that cursedly determined pack of vampires who were chasing after him now, obviously in the mood for an early dinner.

His plans having absolutely nothing to do with becoming the main course at a vampire feast, Ethan had done—and, blast the lot of them, was still doing—the only intelligent thing. He had fled, hoping that the vampires didn't know more of the town's backways than he did.

Uh-oh. A fence up ahead. Hadn't been there the last time he'd cut through this way. Ridiculous to put up a fence in an alley, particularly when someone really, *really* might need to put on a burst of speed.

Ethan took a deep breath, leaped, grabbed the top of the fence with both hands, and scrambled over, landing with a jolt on the other side. Breathless, he caught his balance and raced on, dashing about a corner—then stopped, listening . . .

Silence.

He glanced warily back around the corner. No one . . . He waited a moment more. Still no one.

"At last!"

Ethan stepped out of the alley, back onto the main

street of Sunnydale's downtown, which, at this hour, was nearly deserted. A car full of teenagers drove by, windows open and music blaring. He winced.

"Maybe they'll do for appetizers, instead of me."

Whether through luck or some remnant of good fortune smiling down on him, he really did seem to have outdistanced his pursuers.

Most of them. To Ethan's horror, two vampires, evidently the only ones who had been able to make it over that fence, raced out of the alley, then stopped, heads turning fiercely left, right.

They couldn't *scent* him, could they? Slipping into the narrow protection of a storefront doorway, Ethan held his breath, willing himself to be as unnoticeable as possible.

"Left," one vampire growled suddenly.

Ethan dared not even let out a sigh of relief. He stood frozen as they ran off, away from him, and kept going. Just to be on the safe side, he waited until they totally were out of sight before stepping back out onto the street.

"Idiots. You'd think they'd have better hunting instincts than that."

Not, of course, that he was complaining. But he did have to wonder if any vampire had starved to death from ineptitude.

Ethan dusted himself off as best he could and did his best to tuck the torn jacket sleeve back in place, then checked his watch under the light of the nearest streetlamp.

Nine-thirty. The Slayer should be starting her patrol right about now.

"Which makes life much easier for me."

No more vampire surprises, for one thing. For another . . . Rupert knew that the creature, whatever it was, was in town. So the dear Ripper was bound to have his Slayer tracking it, trying to make sure that the creature was declawed and harmless.

"And so, all I need do is track her in turn." Ethan grinned. "And—ta-da—I find the creature myself."

Granted, he had no real reason to want the creature, whatever it might turn out to be. That much work for an uncertain result wasn't his style at all. Except, of course, for the fact that it interested him and just might be useful.

And, of course, for the fact that his very being in town annoyed Rupert.

Ethan's grin widened. *Two very good reasons for doing anything: curiosity—and petty revenge.*

"Here, vampy," Buffy called into the night as she stalked, not really expecting an answer. "Here, vampy vampy vampy."

Nope. Nothing. The entire night had been dead, slayagewise. For all the action she was seeing, she could just as well have stayed home with some boring textbook. Or gone over to the Bronze and heard the lamer bands, who had mercifully all been scheduled for early in the evening. So far, the entire vampire population of Sunnydale seemed to be lying low.

Buffy had brought up the weirdness factor with her Watcher once again this afternoon, but once again Giles had just muttered the usual bit about not letting her guard down, no matter what lulls might occur. And he'd once again shot down her theory, that the korred was causing it, because a korred shouldn't have much influence on a demon.

"But it's not like Giles hasn't been wrong before."

Ugly thought. Watchers were supposed to have all the answers.

"Yeah, and Slayers are supposed to follow orders and not have a social life, and . . . I'll take him not having all the answers."

And Giles *had* added a sort of half-suggestion, something to do with magnetic forces or surges in the earth or the Hellmouth. In other words, something perfectly . . . well, one couldn't apply "normal" here. Just say that even the Hellmouth might have a down cycle and leave it at that.

Whoa. Suddenly she felt, she *knew,* that something was behind her. All her muscles went tense, but Buffy pretended not to be reacting at all. Staking vamps was always nice, but this was what she was really hunting tonight—the korred. In the end, that was all their korred-extermination ideas had boiled down to—her luring the thing to the outskirts of town and then dumping it. Giles figured that once she got it away from the Hellmouth itself, it would get bored, and just wander away back to wherever it came from. Back to sucking off tree rats and the occasional larger animal.

"Just as a bear goes back to berries and roots," Giles had said, "when living prey isn't available."

"When they don't have people food to munch on," Buffy had retorted.

Buffy still wasn't convinced getting rid of the korred would be that easy, but killing it seemed a severe long shot. Not one of Giles's books—and he had a *lot*—mentioned a surefire way to kill a korred.

"They're like the cockroaches of supernatural critters," Buffy muttered.

So, lure and ditch. And hope it got the message and went home.

"Which would be a good thing. 'Cause the only dancing I want to do is tonight at the Bronze, when the Dingoes kick some serious musical butt."

She turned around.

Cordelia stopped short in the middle of the sidewalk. "You promise?"

"I promise."

"No, really promise me. This is *important*, Xander."

Xander sighed, slinging his arm around Cordelia's shoulders. "I promise. No geek dancing whatsoever tonight. I shall be totally geek-dance free. I will limit myself to the moves you have personally preapproved. I will not forget myself, I will not do happy feet, I will not shame, embarrass, or otherwise humiliate you in front of the collected school population."

Cordelia sighed. "I don't know why I even bother. You'll get on the dance floor and all your geek genes will just take over."

She snuggled closer under his arm, since there was no one around to see them. "It's lucky for you nobody really expects you to dance well."

"Yay, lucky me." Glancing at his watch, Xander

made a face. "And late me. Late both of us. The Dingoes were supposed to go on at 9:45, and I promised Will that we'd be there to cheer them on. There's no way we're going to make it in time."

"Well, I'm sorry. But it's not my fault that *some-one* dressed to clash with my outfit. Didn't I tell you to check in with me before getting dressed? And by the time we got here, all the good parking spaces were taken, and I had to park wa-a-ay away, so that I don't even know if my car will still be there when this is all over—"

"Shhh . . ."

"Don't shhh me! Your dancing we can overlook, but outfits are—"

"Cordelia, shut up! Did you hear that?"

Cordelia stopped. "No, what? What did you hear?"

Xander shook his head, dropping his arm from around Cordelia and turning slowly. They were still a couple of blocks from the Bronze, well into the part of town that the Sunnydale Chamber of Commerce didn't put on their friendly little brochures or up on the web page. It might not have been impressive by Los Angeles' standards, but the row of empty warehouses and storefronts could wig a person out even if one didn't know what normally skulked around after dark.

And if one did . . .

"Got a stake handy?"

Cordelia had already pulled a can of pepper spray from her bag. "Give me credit, Harris. Like I'm going out at night in Sunnydale without protection?"

Since the summer spent subbing for the Slayer, they had all gotten better about carrying stakes and crosses—or at least a can of spray. They weren't much better at using them, but at least they had a fighting chance now when the Slayer wasn't around.

"So what's with the waiting?" Cordelia whispered after a few seconds. "If there's something out there, why doesn't it attack already? I swear—"

"There! Listen. Do you hear it now?"

Cordelia listened, trying to filter out the noise of the cars on the main road a couple of blocks over, and the muted bass coming through the concrete block walls of the Bronze.

"Yeah. Like humming, kind of. That's weird—" She stopped, her brain working half a step quicker than Xander's. "Oh no . . ."

Xander realized the truth just then, his eyes widening in horror as the humming grew louder. "Oh *yes*. Cordy, cover your ears! Run!"

But it was already far too late for that.

CHAPTER 14

Ethan Rayne stopped short, staring at the two figures dimly lit by the streetlamp half a block ahead. *Now, that is odd. Even for Sunnyhell.* For one quick second, he'd thought that they were messing around, or perhaps trying to be romantic, dancing in the moonlight. *If you could call that dancing.* But there was nothing even remotely romantic about those gyrations. It was, in fact, almost as though . . .

As though they were being somehow *forced* to dance. And, Ethan realized sharply, it was not being done for some typically stupid teenager rationale, such as an initiation rite or a dare. No, he knew the smell of magic when it was in the air, and it was heavy here. The victims had no choice about this.

And, more to the point, whatever was making them dance was nothing human.

A quick survey of the area showed him that the

creature holding them captive was, from its size and—he sniffed the air—aroma, most likely the creature he had been looking for.

Ethan quickly squashed the foolish impulse to go closer to investigate. Anything strong enough to catch two teenagers like that was doubtlessly strong enough to catch any adult within reach as well. *I won't dance, don't ask me,* he thought, and decided that he could see just as clearly from a distance. *Yes, and make more leisurely plans about what—*

Well, now, look who else is here! Ethan hastily slid backward into a shadow. The Slayer, who had been in front of him a block and a wrong turn ago, passed right by him, apparently oblivious to mere mortal bystanders. In her casual skirt and top, she could have been any young girl walking home from a date.

Any young girl, he amended his thought, *who carries a virtual arsenal against the undead.* Two stakes were tucked into her waistband, and another one was strapped to the side of her left boot, like some gunslinger's holster. And he would guess that what he could see was only the tip of the iceberg. *So to speak.*

But if her weapons were dangerous, the irritation in her voice was lethal. Ethan was only thankful it wasn't directed at him. Entertained by the running monologue she was having with herself, he followed, perhaps a little closer than he should have for self-preservation's sake, in order to better eavesdrop.

And watch what was surely just about to happen. *Ten pounds on the Slayer,* he thought to himself.

Fifteen if she knows those poor idiots the thing has trapped.

"You so owe me, Giles," Buffy fumed. "'Cause this has been one totally wasted night. I mean, it follows me for what, a week? And then when I want it—nowhere to be found. Proof positive, should it be required, that the mad giggler is definitely of the male variety."

Her boots made flat slapping noises on the pavement, echoing from one end of the street to the other. She had gotten to know this part of town like the back of her hand. The Bronze was just a couple of blocks over, but the rest of the area verged on abandoned. Prime vamp hunting grounds, since people who hung here tended to not cause a fuss if they up and disappeared. On a normal Sunnydale night, she could stake two, three, easy just on one pass.

Tonight? She had been on patrol for hours and hadn't seen anything even remotely supernatural. No vamps, no stalker—not even that chicken thing, the basi-whatever, that had Giles so interested. It was starting to irk. And it was especially irksome, considering that she had seriously missed most of the Battle of the Bands by now.

"It's not like I mind it when saving the world trashes my social life," she said, practicing her rant before she tried it out on Giles tomorrow. "But when there's no world saveage, then it becomes seriously unfine. And furthermore—"

The fine hairs on the back of her neck rose, and goose bumps formed along the bare skin of her arms.

"Okay. That's a little more like it."

Pulling a stake out, in case it was just a vamp or two with lousy timing, she moved around the corner, keeping her back to the faded-brick wall of the building.

But what she saw, illuminated by a streetlight that somehow hadn't burned out or been smashed, was not vampirish.

That didn't mean it wasn't ugly.

Well, sure, Xander had never been one of the great dancers of all times—but this was, like, the Ultimate Geek in Action, arms flailing wildly, legs kicking, stomping like he was trying to wipe out a whole army of ants. For a second, Buffy thought that maybe he was being deliberately dorky, like maybe trying to get Cordy to laugh.

But the expression on her friend's face wasn't the normal having-fun-getting-funky grin Xander usually wore. And Cordelia was definitely not in the mood for laughs. She was dancing, too, and managing to move with a little more grace, but tears of fear and exhaustion ran down her face. Her eye makeup had smeared too, and there was no way Cordelia, even a Cordelia possessed by a demon, wouldn't have fixed that by now.

Unless, of course, she and Xander couldn't stop.

"Oh, great," Buffy muttered, realizing what was going on. "How'd you get ahead of me?"

Still in the shadows, Buffy scanned the street

behind her two friends. *There. Yes!* The korred. Had to be. Red eyes, goat feet, dark spikey hair sticking out all over the stocky body and skinny legs, just like the picture Willow had shown her.

It was butt ugly. And getting way too much enjoyment from watching Xander and Cordelia twist like marionettes handled by someone with Tourette's.

"Yep, gotta be an evil whatwhosit. Nothing on the side of good could watch that without cringing."

Pushing away from the wall, Buffy did the Slayer thing. Which opened, natch, with her traditional battle cry:

"Hey, Nair-impaired! What's with the dance party?"

Okay, so it lacked the impact of Xena's weird yodel thing. But Buffy hadn't had time to prepare anything specific to korreds. And besides, it worked. Mister ugly swung around to face her, and Xander and Cordy fell like somebody cut their strings, collapsing into a sweaty, panting pile.

The two of them leaned helplessly against each other, trying to catch their breath. Xander managed to lift his head up enough to see Buffy, and made like he was trying to give her a cheery wave. But he obviously couldn't even raise his hand.

"Hey . . . Buffster," he said, taking in a huge gasp of air.

"Thank God . . . you got here." Cordelia was struggling not to be so uncool as to pant. "I broke a heel . . . dancing to that . . . stupid thing!"

But Buffy was too busy sizing up her new opponent to pay any real attention.

"Come on," she taunted it, "I'm what you're interested in, right? Well, come and take a piece of me. If you think you can!"

The korred grinned evilly at the Slayer, showing disgustingly yellow teeth, and giggled madly.

"And quit with that! I mean, you sound like a moron!"

Buffy stared at the creature, remembering Giles's words about taking in the details for future reference. "You're not so scary in the light. Still ugly, though."

Not a word from the korred. Maybe it couldn't talk? *Or it only speaks what, Cornish?* But it was making some sort of humming sound, almost pretty, actually . . .

Oh. Right. She couldn't hear it before 'cause it had been directed at Xander and Cordelia. But now it was trying to enchant her. "That is so not on the game plan, pal. All right, Giles. Here goes. And this had better work!"

She raised her hands to her ears, as though to check that her earrings were still in place, and then, with a quick leap and kick that caught the startled korred square in the stomach, Buffy attacked.

Ethan, in the shadows, watched for a while out of sheer aesthetic interest, then winced at a particularly solid blow to what, in a human male, would have been extremely bad news, feeling a flash of sympathy for the korred. He gauged which way the fight was going, then gave a silent little sigh of regret. His fifteen pounds were safe.

I've been on the receiving end of those kicks, my odd little magical fellow. You'll pardon me if I don't wait around for her to finish with you, and perhaps find me.

No, if the Slayer were ever to discover that he had been there, even if she believed that he hadn't had a thing to do with this particular setup . . . It would get ugly. For him, that was. Enough, Ethan decided, was enough. The creature wasn't worth that. He would annoy Rupert some other time.

Moving with a catlike grace, and whistling his own tune quite cheerfully, Ethan Rayne left the scene.

After the first few blows sent it staggering, the korred was almost too stunned to fight back. *This wasn't supposed to happen!* The—the mouse didn't ever turn on the cat!

More singing, it decided. *Stronger. Louder.* Even this . . . this no-longer-so-fascinating human female wouldn't be able to resist. It would see her dance all night, consuming her bright swirls of energy until there was nothing left but a meat shell.

As it sang, the two other humans huddled on the ground together shivered, twitching, crying out, and the korred grinned.

But the girl who faced it never even flinched.

"Come on, ugly!" she taunted. "Afraid of a li'l ole Slayer?"

Her voice was oddly flat, even for a human, in a

way it hadn't been before. It was as though . . . as though she couldn't hear herself speaking! She had done something, it realized. Something to her ears, so that sound couldn't reach her. And if she couldn't hear herself, she couldn't hear it! The korred's snaggle-toothed grin faded as it realized that its song magic was useless.

But then its lips drew up in a new snarl, this one even uglier than the grin it had been wearing before. It was not so dependent upon magic as this human child would believe. She wanted a fight? Then fight it would!

Buffy drew back for an instant. Judging from what were probably expressions of dismay and anger crossing that ugly face, the creature must have just realized that she couldn't hear it.

Whoops. So much for the element of it-not-knowing.

Snarling, the korred drew itself up, the look in its little red eyes glazing over, as though it were concentrating. . . .

"Oh no."

Willow had been right. It could change its size. The magic it had been throwing at her must have been redirected into itself, because it grew swiftly to almost twice its original size. Twice the mass, three times as ugly.

Now looming over her, it licked its lips with a long black tongue, and lunged.

"Oh no you don't, ugly!"

This, Buffy could handle. She was pretty good at hand-to-hand, if she did say so herself. And she hadn't had any exercise that night, thanks to the scarcity of vampires. But as they grappled, one claw-fisted hand swiped at the side of her head, coming away with a chunk of blond hair—and a wax earplug she had inserted at the beginning of the fight. Crying out in pain, blood running down the side of her face, Buffy disengaged and fell back a few paces, out of its reach.

Great. Well, that didn't work, Giles, did it?

No time to worry about that. She launched herself at the creature again, getting in a few good punches and kicks before the korred could start singing at her again. But it *was* singing already, kind of: a thin, eerie melody—and the magic in that reedy humming was so strong it made goose bumps rise all over her body.

"Weird tune," she said, falling back and panting. "But I gotta tell you, the Dingoes woulda whupped your hide, too."

And then the magic reached her, and Buffy felt her limbs start to twitch in the need to move, as though fire was shooting through her veins and making every nerve scream for movement. *Like some kind of killer itch that had to be scratched or I will explode . . .*

But Buffy Summers was the Slayer. And that meant that she didn't go down before anything. Not vampires, not principals, and certainly not some overgrown Chia Pet!

"All right, ugly, if I *have* to dance, let's do it right."

West Side Story. She and her mom had rented it

one night, one of their weepy popcorn chick-flick fests. That was the way, those gang guys who danced their fights—*kick! And punch! Use the music to keep time—whirl and drop, then up in a leaping kick* . . .

Martial arts had come easily to her, the moves Giles drummed into her head becoming instinctive reactions. But before she had been the Slayer, Buffy had been a cheerleader. And before cheerleading, there had been those years at ballet school and ice skating.

Nothing is ever forgotten. It just hangs around in your memory until one day it's needed again.

Okay, so her ballet teacher might never have intended for a *grand écart* to be used this offensively, but it worked quite nicely.

The fight moved out into the middle of the street, the korred using sheer brute strength to keep the Slayer from taking it down. It was impressive, the mass of muscle hidden in that misshapen body. But she was unstoppable as well, drawing on its own power—the power of music—to fuel her own assault.

"Make me miss the Battle of the Bands, will you? Stalk me like some little dateless creep? Try to take on my friends? I so don't *think* so."

The music faltered, and she got in one good hard kick that sent the korred staggering back against a wall. Another kick snapped its head back. But when she tried to close, to finish it once and for all, those red eyes glowered at her, and those teeth snapped at her arm, forcing her to pull back out of range.

"Okay. So, we do this the old-fashioned way."

Gathering herself, Buffy swayed into the music and made one last, high, side kick that a Rockette would have envied—the heel of her boot catching the korred flat in the throat with a nasty, wet, crushing noise.

For a long while, neither she nor it moved. Then the korred made one last pitiful noise, grabbed at its destroyed larynx, and ran.

Buffy dropped into an exhausted crouch and glanced over to where Xander and Cordelia were slowly untangling themselves from each other. She forced a weary grin.

"Next time," she suggested, "try to make it to the Bronze. The music's way better."

CHAPTER 15

BUFFY THE VAMPIRE SLAYER

Buffy stalked into Sunnydale High School the next morning, past teens on step stools pulling down the Battle of the Bands banners, and on into the library. "I can't believe it!"

Giles, a small stack of books clutched in his arms, stared at her in alarm. "What? What went wrong? Did the korred—"

"Oh, I kicked the korred but good. Nailed the critter right in the throat and stopped that stupid giggle once and for all. You would have been proud of me, Giles. But I can't believe I missed the entire Battle of the Bands!"

"Ah. Well. Yes." Giles reshelved the books one at a time. "One must have one's priorities, I suppose."

"Giles! You don't understand—Hey! Where is everyone? The place is, like, empty."

Giles looked around. "The student teachers, you

mean? The invasion seems to be over. They're being sent on to the next school in the program."

"Awww." Buffy flopped down at the long table. "No more groupies following you around."

"A situation I shall not miss."

"Right. Of course." She waved a hand as the library door opened. "Hey, Will! Giles has lost his admirers."

"Oh. Sorry, Giles."

That was definitely a "humph" from Giles, who pushed his glasses further up on his nose and turned away, resolutely ignoring them.

Willow sat down at the table, across from Buffy, looking so determinedly cheerful that Buffy asked, "Didn't win?"

"No. The Dingoes' *Ate My Babies* came in second."

"Hey, that's still cool! Money prize, too, right?"

Willow nodded, a real smile showing up. "And Oz said the Dingoes picked up another gig, too, 'cause of some guy hearing them. Which is cool." Willow blinked. "But what happened last night? I mean, the korred and all?"

"Oh, not much," Buffy said, doing the extreme nonchalant. "Went stalking the korred, korred found Xander and Cordy instead. Plan failed—and we have got to talk about that Giles, 'cause I lost my best earring—and I did what I do. Which was pretty impressive, if I do say so myself."

"Yeah, that's about right," Xander said from the doorway, and followed that with an enormous yawn and a stretch. "That dancercize class last night was a killer."

"It was terrible," Cordelia added, slipping past Xander to join Buffy and Willow at the table. "I mean, my makeup was smearing. And my hair was—I'm so glad no one saw me. Except you, of course, Buffy. But thankfully you don't count."

"Gee, Cordy," Buffy commented, "you always know exactly what to say."

"But . . . the korred," Willow said. "What about it? Where is it?"

"Good point, Will. Giles, I didn't actually kill the korred. Is it gonna come back?"

Giles turned around, taking his glasses off and tapping them against his lips thoughtfully. "Well. Although you did not kill the korred, you did effectively silence it. If your guess is correct, it has fled from the vicinity of the Hellmouth." He gestured with his folded glasses, deep into Giles Lecture Mode. "An injured earth being such as the korred will rush off from the site of its wounding and return to earth."

"Meaning," Willow translated, "that it won't stop running till it hits a mountain and burrows back in."

"Exactly."

"OK, now what?" Xander asked.

"Now," said a familiar, faintly accented voice, "I must congratulate you."

Giles stiffened. "Panner. You're up early."

"Not particularly. There seems to be very little time to sleep in Sunnydale. So much going on."

Panner gave them such an elegant bow that Buffy stared and Cordelia straightened up. "But I am afraid that my work here, as the saying goes, is done."

Giles wasn't impressed. "Is it?"

"My dear Rupert, there is no need to bristle at me! I told you that I was not here to impede your work. Merely to record it."

"Oh," Cordelia said suddenly. "A Watcher's Watcher."

Buffy turned to glare at her, since Giles was busy glaring at Panner.

"And . . . ?" Giles prodded.

"And what I have seen here is quite the effective team. A bit . . . eccentric in its operation, perhaps, but effective."

"And . . . ?" Giles continued to prod. "What else?"

Panner smiled. Actually, truly smiled. And his face didn't crack. Buffy took a minute to marvel at that.

"Ah, Rupert, you always had a rather distressing tendency toward paranoia. But yes, there was more to this visit. You, my dear," he added, dipping his head to Willow, who promptly reddened. "I was intrigued by stories I had heard of the Slayerettes. Most specifically, of a young woman who just might have the intellect and aptitude to be recruited."

"Recruited . . . ?" Willow's voice was barely audible. "As a . . . Watcher? Oh no, you've made a mistake, a big mistake, I mean I'm not—"

"Precisely what I decided. You are a bright young woman, young lady, with a great deal of potential, but not quite ready for the rigors of being a Watcher."

"And maybe I don't want to *be* a Watcher!" Willow retorted, then reddened still further, looking at Giles. "I mean, I don't know, I . . ."

"No matter." Panner's voice was almost light. "Rupert, I must say that it was a pleasure seeing you again—and learning for myself how well you and your Slayer are doing your jobs. And now I fear that I must say good-bye."

"Have a safe journey."

Judging from the expression on Giles's face, that was far from what he'd wanted to say. Panner hesitated a moment, then clearly changed his mind. With a second bow, the older man turned and left.

It wasn't that the air suddenly got cleaner or anything, but everyone breathed a little better when the door closed behind him.

Then everyone turned to stare at Willow.

"Uh, the korred," Willow said hastily, before anyone could say anything to her. "What happens to it now? I mean, once it goes to earth? Does it heal?"

Giles sat down beside her, a scholar's enthusiasm back in his eyes. "That is an interesting question. One historian proposed that when such a creature is wounded . . ."

Buffy rolled her eyes, and tuned out with the ease of long practice. Bad guy was defeated, blah blah blah, no need to learn more. That's what Slayers had Watchers for, to do the Knowing Stuff thing.

Judging from their dazed expressions, Xander and Cordelia had lost the gist of Giles's ramble already.

Only Willow appeared really interested. Buffy sighed. This could go on for some time.

Time! Right! Buffy jumped up. "I hate to break up this meeting of the Mythology Debating Club, but some of us really need to get to class."

"Hey, class," Xander echoed. "Right. Good idea. I can get some quality sleep there. Only joking!" he added when Giles frowned.

"'Do you want fries with that?'" Willow asked, then put on her best innocent expression when Xander looked sideways at her.

"Ah. Well." Giles put his glasses back on and stood up. "To quote the Bard: All's well that ends well."

"Well?" Cordelia asked, standing up. "For your information, I broke the heel of my best boots last night! That's not 'well.'"

Smiling faintly, Rupert Giles watched his Slayer and her Slayerettes file out of the library, chattering together. *Almost like normal teenagers.* When they were gone, he breathed a sigh of relief.

Another monster had been defeated. All the visitors have left. Panner was gone. No further word from Ethan. The student teachers, that ridiculous Librarian Posse, had ended their stay at Sunnydale High School. The library was his again.

Exuding satisfaction, he returned to reshelving the pile of books. Then he stopped, frowning. *Wasn't there another one in this pile?*

Sitting in class, Willow opened her notebook, and scrunched down in her chair. And then she reached back into her knapsack and pulled out a small leather-bound book. Hiding it within the larger notebook, she flipped open to a page and happily began reading Giles's journal.

It is a library, isn't it? And one is supposed to check stuff out, and learn from it, right?

ABOUT THE AUTHORS

Laura Anne Gilman is executive editor at NAL, where she works on mysteries, science fiction, horror, fantasy, and New Age books. Giving up sleep, she is also the author of a dozen well-received short stories, some of which can be found in the anthologies *Did You Say Chicks?*, *Highwaymen: Robbers and Rogues,* and *Blood Thirst: 100 Years of Vampire Fiction,* where she shares space with Woody Allen and Bram Stoker, among others. She lives in New Jersey with her husband Peter, cat Indiana, and a v.90 modem named gofaster! She can be reached at www.sff.net/people/LauraAnne.Gilman

Josepha Sherman is a fantasy writer and folklorist whose books include the dark urban fantasy *Son of Darkness;* the *Star Trek* novels *Vulcan's Forge* and the forthcoming *Vulcan's Heart,* cowritten with Susan Shwartz; the *Highlander* novel *The Captive Soul;* the *Xena* book *Xena: All I Need to Know I Learned from the Warrior Princess, by Gabrielle, as Translated by Josepha Sherman;* and the folklore volume *Merlin's Kin: World Tales of the Hero Magician.* She is a member of the Authors Guild, SFWA, and the American Folklore Society. It goes without saying that she is a fan of *Buffy!* She can be reached at www.sff.net/people/Josepha.Sherman.

"They say young people don't learn anything in high school nowadays, but I've learned to be afraid."
—*Xander*

BUFFY
THE VAMPIRE
SLAYER™

THE POSTCARDS

Buffy Summers may have missed picture day at Sunnydale High, but now you can get your own stash of all-new Slayer snapshots.

Twenty-two official, full-color photos from the hit show—all packed into one postcard gift book.

Available February 1999

POCKET BOOKS

Published by Pocket Books

2058

BUFFY

THE VAMPIRE

SLAYER™

"You're not friends.
You'll never be friends.
You'll be in love until it kills you both."
—Spike, "Lovers Walk"

The Essential Angel

A special posterbook packed with photos
of Angel, and featuring signature quotes
and detailed info about Buffy's favorite
vampire with a soul.

Available in April 1999

Published by Pocket Books

**POCKET
BOOKS**

2069